"I'm calling security."

Mari's threat didn't stop Bryce. It was the sight of her hazel eyes, awash with tears, that froze him in his tracks.

Were the tears a ruse, or evidence of her compassion?

He didn't know, but an impulse he couldn't control propelled him forward, arms open. Wrapping them around her, he pulled her close. A flood of images flashed through his mind. Caught off guard, he did his best to ignore the unwanted memories. He struggled to keep his head clear. Where had his objectivity gone? She was a suspect and he was here to question her, not to hold her in his arms.

His silent lecture wasn't taking hold.

"It's okay," he murmured.

His voice jerked her head up. Her eyes met his, and his mouth went dry. A giant fist squeezed the breath from his lungs. Neither of them moved, neither blinked.

And he tried to remember why kissing her would be a very, very bad idea.

D0645935

Dear Reader,

It's spring, love is in the air…and what better way to celebrate than by taking a break with Silhouette Special Edition? We begin the month with *Treasured*, the conclusion to Sherryl Woods's MILLION DOLLAR DESTINIES series. Though his two brothers have been successfully paired off, Ben Carlton is convinced he's "destined" to go it alone. But the brooding, talented young man is about to meet his match in a beautiful gallery owner—courtesy of fate…plus a little help from his matchmaking aunt.

And Pamela Toth concludes the MERLYN COUNTY MIDWIVES series with *In the Enemy's Arms*, in which a detective trying to get to the bottom of a hospital black-market drug investigation finds himself in close contact with his old high school flame, now a beautiful M.D.—she's his prime suspect! And exciting new author Lynda Sandoval (look for her Special Edition novel *One Perfect Man*, coming in June) makes her debut and wraps up the LOGAN'S LEGACY Special Edition prequels, all in one book—*And Then There Were Three*. Next, Christine Flynn begins her new miniseries, THE KENDRICKS OF CAMELOT, with *The Housekeeper's Daughter*, in which a son of Camelot—Virginia, that is—finds himself inexplicably drawn to the one woman he can never have. Marie Ferrarella moves her popular CAVANAUGH JUSTICE series into Special Edition with *The Strong Silent Type*, in which a female detective finds her handsome male partner somewhat less than chatty. But her determination to get him to talk quickly morphs into a determination to…get him. And in Ellen Tanner Marsh's *For His Son's Sake*, a single father trying to connect with the son whose existence he just recently discovered finds in the free-spirited Kenzie Daniels a woman they could *both* love.

So enjoy! And come back next month for six heartwarming books from Silhouette Special Edition.

Happy reading!

Gail Chasan
Senior Editor

Please address questions and book requests to:
Silhouette Reader Service
U.S.: 3010 Walden Ave., P.O. Box 1325, Buffalo, NY 14269
Canadian: P.O. Box 609, Fort Erie, Ont. L2A 5X3

In the Enemy's Arms

PAMELA TOTH

Silhouette

SPECIAL EDITION

Published by Silhouette Books

America's Publisher of Contemporary Romance

Special thanks and acknoledgment are given
to Pamela Toth for her contribution to the
MERLYN COUNTY MIDWIVES series.

With appreciation to all those heroes
who protect the rest of us from real enemies,
and to the families who support them.

SILHOUETTE BOOKS

ISBN 0-373-24610-2

IN THE ENEMY'S ARMS

Visit Silhouette Books at www.eHarlequin.com

Printed in U.S.A.

Chapter One

"What is *he* doing here?"

As Mari Bingham peeled off her gloves, she glared at the detective staring back at her through the glass divider. It seemed to Mari as though every time she turned around, even here at the midwifery clinic where she was the director, she noticed Bryce Collins watching her. If not for his gold shield, she would have filed a stalking complaint against him.

"He's been waiting to talk to you." The receptionist lowered her voice, her expression concerned. "Is everything okay, Dr. Bingham?"

"Of course, Heather. Everything's fine." Mari dredged up a smile. She'd been called in to the clinic at 2:00 a.m. and it was now midmorning. Even though she was the director, she still saw patients. Mari considered the joy of bringing a healthy baby into the world well worth a few hours of lost sleep, but this delivery had been a long one and the last few weeks had been difficult for her.

Mari had been meaning to confront Detective Collins, but not here, not now, and certainly not without a shot of caffeine to hone her senses.

In her search for decent coffee, she had come straight from the birthing room without bothering to freshen up first. She must look awful—her face pale and shiny, her hair falling from its hasty bun and her light green scrubs stained and wrinkled.

From previous experience, she knew all too well that neither a carefully made-up face nor a freshly laundered outfit would have lessened the defensiveness she always felt around the man advancing on her now with the determination of a cougar stalking a deer. He had been after her for weeks.

Despite the rumors and speculation surrounding Mari, she refused to cooperate and play the role of prey. She just wanted the investigation to be over, the real criminals caught and her reputation cleared.

"Please show the detective to my office," she told Heather as Bryce narrowly avoided tripping over a toddler pushing a tiny grocery cart across the waiting room. "I'll be there in a minute."

Mari didn't care how long he'd been cooling his heels. He should know from his last attempt at interrogating her here that the Foster Midwifery Clinic was a busy place. Besides, she desperately needed some coffee and a bagel, if there were any left over from the morning break. Except for a few of the tiny breath mints she always carried with her, she hadn't eaten a thing since dinner last night.

Let Heather deal with Bryce's intimidation tactics for the moment. It would be good practice for the girl.

As Mari made her escape, she swallowed a yawn. It was no surprise that she hadn't been sleeping well, even on the few nights that one of her patients didn't go into labor at 2:00 a.m. Worrying about who might be evil enough to steal drugs from the clinic and then let someone else—her—take the blame was wearing Mari down. The last thing she needed today was another visit from Bryce Collins.

She knew he had stopped loving her a long time ago, but was it possible that he still resented her enough to send her to prison—even if it was for something she hadn't done?

Detective Collins had been studying Mari through the glass divider. He watched the receptionist with the eye-popping blue hair give Mari the no doubt unwelcome news of his presence. As he got to his feet, Mari's gaze collided with his. Even with her spine stiffened, she looked tired.

Was her obvious fatigue merely a by-product of her chosen profession? Becoming a doctor, an obstetrician, had been a goal he hadn't been willing to support. In fact, when they were younger, Bryce had done everything in his power to dissuade her from pursuing a career in medicine. Judging from her current wilted appearance, it appeared that her job was taking its toll.

Grudgingly Bryce supposed the investigation—*his* investigation—might also be partly to blame. Was a guilty conscience keeping her awake at night? Did she feel sorry for the victims of the switched pain medication or was it merely the fear of getting caught supplying drugs to the black market that dimmed her normal sparkle?

His determination to find answers was the reason he'd spent the last hour waiting to see her. He'd been surrounded by chattering mommies, fussing babies and whiny toddlers. One of the latter had just wiped a mashed-up cookie on the knee of Bryce's slacks.

Given a choice, he would rather be chasing a suspect through a dark alley full of pit bulls.

Instead of waiting for him, Mari walked away. He nearly ran down two little kids when he chased after her, swearing under his breath.

With her clipboard clutched to her chest, the blue-haired receptionist headed him off while Mari disappeared around a corner. Biting back his impatience, Bryce glanced at the girl's name tag.

"Heather, I told you that I need to speak to Dr. Bingham," he said, doing his best to soften his request with a smile.

"She asked that you wait in her office. I'll take

you there right now and the doctor will be with you in just a little while.''

So far, he had nothing to show for the morning that was rapidly slipping away except for the dried cookie on his knee. "Great," he replied, his annoyance oozing out. "It's not as if I've got anything better to do with my time."

Below the silver hoop that pierced Heather's brow, her black-rimmed eyes widened. With a huff of annoyance, she spun on her heel, leaving him no choice but to follow.

The case was getting a fair amount of publicity and he had grown up in Merlyn County, so people recognized him. Today he ignored the curious glances of the patients and the disapproving stares from some of the clinic staff as he focused on getting his interview with his number-one person of interest.

The receptionist opened the door marked Marigold Bingham, M.D., Director and stepped aside. Heather's frosty expression didn't thaw, but it actually went rather well with her icy-blue hair.

"You can wait in here," she said. "Do you want coffee?"

Whatever they served here at the clinic had to be an improvement on the bilge at the station. For an instant he was tempted, but he didn't want to be distracted.

"No, thanks," he said reluctantly. "I'm fine."

She must have been worried that he might snoop through Mari's paperwork, because she hesitated with her hand on the doorjamb. It was only when he sat down facing the cluttered desk and withdrew his notebook from his jacket pocket that she left.

Unfortunately for Dr. Bingham, the obvious loyalty of her staff was no indication whatsoever of her guilt or innocence. The grim fact was that someone who worked here was stealing Orcadol, a popular and powerful new prescription painkiller, and selling it on the street. From a personal point of view, and because Bryce had known her for so long, he was reluctant to believe that Mari could be involved in something as despicable as drug trafficking. As a detective with the Merlyn County Sheriff's Department, it was his sworn duty to follow the trail of evidence that pointed relentlessly in her direction.

He scrubbed one hand over his jaw, feeling its roughness. He needed a shave. A stakeout on an unrelated case had gotten him up at dawn, but the perps never showed. Sometimes his job sucked.

Sheriff Remington, a crusader against illegal drugs, was growing impatient with Bryce's lack of progress in the Orcadol case. Just this morning the sheriff had asked Bryce for a status report, but there had been damn little to say.

Over the course of his career, Bryce had witnessed time and again the damage caused by drugs; the broken, wasted lives, the crimes committed in order to feed habits gone out of control, the families ripped apart and the children hurt by addiction. Was it really possible that someone like Mari, who had taken an oath to save lives, could be responsible for the recent increase of the illegal supply of Orcadol, or Orchid, as it was called on the street?

Nothing surprised Bryce anymore. Greed was a powerful motivator and the word was out that Mari was desperate for money to support the construction of her pet project, a biomedical research facility. The question that ate at him was just how far would she go in order to get it?

Unless Bryce was willing to shoot holes in his own career, he had no choice but to set aside his personal reservations and treat her the same as he would any other suspect. Better in Bryce's opinion to have him be the one investigating her than Merlyn County's other detective, Hank Butler. At least with Bryce on the case, she was less likely to become the victim of sloppy police work, questionable shortcuts or even— it had been whispered but never proven—doctored evidence.

"Dr. Bingham to Neonatal. Dr. Mari Bingham to Neonatal, stat!"

Mari was in her office doorway when she heard the summons to the hospital, which was adjacent to the clinic. Bryce had glanced up and was already halfway to his feet when she stopped.

"Sorry, but I have to see about this," she said, torn between relief at the interruption and concern for whoever needed her. Just this morning Milla Johnson, a midwife at the clinic, had mentioned one of her patients to Mari.

The patient, barely twenty-four weeks pregnant, had been experiencing what she described as twinges. Milla had sounded concerned when she told Mari that the woman's husband was bringing her in for an exam.

"Don't leave!" Bryce snapped before Mari could turn away. "I've been waiting long enough already."

"Apparently not, Detective," she contradicted. "I'll be back as soon as I can." Ignoring his muttered curse, she hurried down the hall toward the sky bridge to the hospital.

Waiting for her was something he had once refused to do, so it only seemed fair for him to cool his heels now.

Bryce dropped back into the chair, flipping once again through his notes and wishing he hadn't refused that cup of coffee. He made a couple of calls on his cell phone, pacing the confines of the small office like a caged bear. Mari still hadn't returned when he was through, so he wandered back out to the main lobby to see if he could get an idea of how long she was going to be held up this time.

Failing to spot Heather, he approached the nurses' station. An older woman wearing a headset was seated at a computer terminal. As she slid back the glass panel, she met his gaze with a smile.

"Is Dr. Bingham back from the hospital yet?"

"I'm afraid not," she replied, glancing at the badge Bryce held out. "One of our patients was brought to the clinic in preterm labor," she continued in a low voice. "The poor thing had to be moved to the neonatal ICU at the hospital when her membranes ruptured. Dr. Bingham is likely to be over there for a while."

Bryce glanced at his watch, unwilling to give up. "I guess I'll grab a sandwich in the cafeteria," he muttered, half to himself. "If you see the doctor before I do, tell her I'm looking for her."

If the woman suspected his reason for seeking Mari out, she didn't let it show. "I'll be sure to do that, Detective. Enjoy your lunch."

When he got back to the clinic after wolfing down a passable meatball sandwich and fries, he approached the same woman again.

"Dr. Bingham is still at the hospital, but you're welcome to go over there and wait," she said, pointing. "The quickest way to get there is right across the sky bridge."

Bryce had been to the hospital on several occasions, but he'd never had a reason to visit the clinic until this investigation had begun. He thanked the woman and headed in the direction she'd indicated.

Babies didn't interest him much, especially wrinkled preemies who looked like tiny bald men, but he needed to make sure that Mari didn't elude him again when she got done. The sheriff had made it clear that the next time he asked about the case, Bryce better have some answers.

"Damn, but I wish he'd stayed where he was for another week or two," Mari muttered as she gazed sadly at the tiny infant. "He's so underdeveloped."

If only his mother had come in sooner, the neonatal team would have had the time for more options. Medications, intravenous fluids and simple bed rest often stopped contractions, but once dilation and effacement of the cervix began, labor nearly always progressed to delivery.

No one replied to Mari's comment.

The hospital, which served three counties, was a level three facility with a fully equipped NICU. In this case, transport to the University of Kentucky research hospital in Lexington might have saved the infant if there had been more time.

Mari was sick at heart, but she needed to be strong and keep her feelings hidden for the rest of the team. Milla, the midwife who had first alerted her to the potential situation and who was also pregnant, was obviously deeply affected by the tragedy.

The neonate had been born with severely underdeveloped lungs, heart and nervous system. Respiratory distress, seizures and intraventricular hemorrhages had contributed to the insurmountable odds. Despite the team's efforts, the end had come quickly.

Mari's throat was clogged with tears she dared not shed when she looked at the impersonal wall clock and conceded defeat. "Thank you, everyone," she added softly.

Milla released a trembling sigh. A hospital resident cursed under his breath and another slammed wordlessly out of the unit.

Mari ignored them, well aware of the frustration, sadness and grief her colleagues experienced whenever this type of thing happened. Before she would be able to share those same emotions and grieve in private for poor Baby Jenkins, she had one more task left to do.

"The parents have to be told," she reminded Milla, willing the young midwife to be strong. "Are you up for it?" If the tears glistening in Milla's eyes were to overflow, Mari wasn't sure she'd able to get through the next few minutes with her own composure intact.

"Yes." Milla blinked rapidly several times. She cleared her throat. "I'm ready."

With a silent nod, Mari led the way to the room where the hopeful parents waited. They may have been praying and were certainly hoping for a miracle to save their son. How many times had it been Mari's duty to break the hearts of people just like this couple?

The hospital and the women's health clinic that her grandmother had been instrumental in developing weren't enough to save these high-risk preemies. What Merlyn County, Kentucky, desperately needed was the new research center that Mari was determined to build.

At the door to the birthing suite, she paused and looked at Milla.

"Okay?" Mari asked. She was fully prepared to intercede if the young midwife was too upset. The parents would need the compassion and support of the medical staff, not their tears.

"Yes, thank you." Milla was dry-eyed, her voice soft but steady.

Allowing her to lead the way, Mari squeezed her eyes shut and composed herself. When she opened them again, she saw Bryce leaning against the far wall with his arms crossed. He had been watching her just like a cat with a mouse.

Her gaze locked with his and her face went hot. She knew he had witnessed her moment of vulnerability, but now she sent him a warning glance before following Milla into the birthing suite and letting the door shut behind her.

The parents were huddled together on the bed, their hands tightly clasped. Mrs. Jenkins's face was red and puffy, but when she saw the two women, her expression brightened.

Mr. Jenkins managed a wobbly smile. "How's our boy doing?" His voice was falsely hearty.

Once again, Mari regretted with all her heart the news they brought.

"I'm so sorry," Milla said softly. "We did every- thing we could, but his problems were too extensive. He didn't make it."

The rest of her explanation was drowned out by Mrs. Jenkins's wrenching sobs.

Outside in the hallway, Bryce waited impatiently for Mari to come out. He wondered how much longer she intended to avoid him.

From behind the closed door, an anguished wail sliced through his thoughts like a surgeon's scalpel. The delivery that Mari had been summoned to must have somehow gone wrong.

No wonder she had looked so grim when he saw her. His presence in the hall probably hadn't even registered with her.

On more than one occasion, it had been his duty to break the bad news to family members about the victim of a fatal accident or a homicide. It was never easy.

He'd always assumed that doctors, like cops, must develop an ability to insulate themselves in some way from the more tragic aspects of their jobs. Mari's hide must be as thick as a concrete retaining wall if she could deal with people's suffering with one hand and dump more Orchid on the streets with the other.

He gritted his teeth and firmed his resolve. If she was guilty, he was going to do everything in his power to bring her down.

Mari knew from sad experience that most of what she and Milla had just told the stunned parents fell on deaf ears. After Milla's initial statement, they had stopped listening while they struggled to absorb the shock. Later on, they would no doubt have questions as they tried to deal with a deluge of guilt they probably didn't deserve.

Leaving Milla to console them as best she could, Mari slipped quietly out of the room. Bryce still lurked in the hall like her own personal black cloud, but she was far too vulnerable to deal with him just yet. Beneath her outward calm, she was raging at fate and circumstance, at whatever force that was so callous it could give parents a precious gift and then coldly, indifferently snatch it back again.

If Bryce were to confront her now, smug and superior in his role of noble law enforcer, she might just jump on him like a crazed lunatic and vent her frustration. If he hadn't hounded her for weeks, snapping at her heels and giving her nightmares, eroding her sleep with his suspicions, might she have come up with a miracle for Baby Jenkins today?

In her doctor's brain, Mari knew she had used every bit of medical expertise and equipment available to her. Deep within her woman's heart, she wondered, as she always did, why every newborn couldn't be saved.

Bryce straightened away from the wall as she went in the other direction. "Dr. Bingham!"

Mari ignored him, walking faster. She needed a moment alone.

"Mari! Wait up."

Without slowing her pace, she waved him away.

"Not now," she called over her shoulder, half expecting him to stop her by force.

To her surprise, he allowed her to escape.

With her teeth tightly clenched, she made a beeline for her office. She shut the door behind her and leaned against it as the tears finally spilled over. For a few moments, she indulged her sorrow and frustration with her knuckles pressed to her mouth to stifle the sounds of her defeat.

Gradually her weeping slowed and she regained control of her emotions. Blindly she grabbed the box of tissues on her desk and blotted her face. When she cried, her nose always got red and her skin turned blotchy. Her eyes probably looked as though she'd been on a three-day bender, so she would have to hide out here for a little while longer.

Someone knocked on the door. Before she could speak, it opened and Bryce leaned in. "You okay?"

"Get out," she snapped.

Instead of complying, he shocked her by coming in and shutting the door behind him. "We need to talk."

Was he blind or just indifferent?

Mari reached for her phone. "I'm calling security," she warned as she lifted the receiver.

Dr. Bingham's threat didn't stop Bryce, who had faced down worse than an unarmed woman holding a wad of damp tissues. It was the sight of her hazel eyes, awash with tears, that froze him in his tracks like a gun trained on his heart.

Were the tears a ruse by a lawbreaker desperate for time? Or was her devastated expression that of a compassionate healer? So many of the people he had interviewed insisted the latter was true.

"Please, Mari." He extended his hand. "Don't call anyone, okay?"

He wasn't sure if it was his words or his tone that stopped her, but he had no intention of giving her time to reconsider. Nor did he intend to offer comfort, but an impulse he couldn't control propelled him forward, arms open. Wrapping them around her, he pulled her close.

Prepared for a struggle, he tucked her head under his chin. As he inhaled the scent of her lemon shampoo, a flood of images flashed through his mind. Caught off guard, he did his best to ignore the unwanted memories, as well as his own spontaneous reaction.

Her slight body stiffened, palms braced against his chest. Barely breathing, he waited for her to jerk away, but instead she sighed, going limp. Before she could sink to the floor, he scooped her up into his arms.

He was shocked at how little she weighed. Had the investigation and his pursuit done this to her?

She slipped her arms around his neck, distracting him, and clung like a child as she cried softly against his chest. The feel of her softly rounded breasts sent awareness pumping through him like a drug. For a moment, he shut his eyes and cuddled her close, wanting to absorb everything about her like a giant sponge.

He struggled to keep his head clear, to keep his lungs working. What the hell was he thinking? Where had his objectivity gone? She was a suspect and he was here to question her, not to hold her in his arms while he mooned over her like a teenager.

His silent lecture wasn't taking hold.

"Shh, baby," he murmured, ignoring his own tap-dancing pulse. "It's okay."

The sound of his voice jerked her head up. Her dark lashes were clumped together. Her eyes were reddened and wet, the skin beneath them blotchy and waxen.

When her lips parted on a tiny sound of protest, his mouth went dry and a giant fist squeezed the breath from his lungs. As they continued to stare at each other, his entire being hummed with awareness.

Neither of them moved, neither blinked. He tried to reason out why kissing her would be a bad idea. A very, very bad idea.

"I think you'd better put me down now." Her voice cracked the silence. Heat of a different type filled his cheeks, but the rest of him went cold at the thought of what he'd nearly done.

"Of course." Gently, he stood her on her feet while he scrambled to regain control of the interview—and his own professionalism.

Her chin went up as she circled the cluttered desk.

After putting the unmistakable barrier between them, she sat down with her hands neatly folded.

"What can I do for you, Detective?" she asked coolly, as though nothing earthshaking had nearly happened.

Bryce was angry at his own weakness, as well as with Mari's ability to manipulate him. Years of professional experience told him she was more likely to slip up and reveal the truth while she was tired and emotionally drained. He couldn't give her the chance to lock her defenses back into place.

"You'll have to come down to the station with me," he replied, deliberately hardening his heart against the sight of her tear-streaked face and dark, wounded eyes. "There are some questions I need to ask you about the drugs being stolen from your clinic."

Chapter Two

It took Mari a moment to process what Bryce had just said. A moment ago, she had thought he might attempt to kiss her.

"You want me to what?" she asked, shocked by his statement. Thank God she was already sitting down or she would have fallen.

"Listen, Mari—" he began.

"Dr. Bingham," she corrected coldly, cutting him off. "What do you expect me to do about my patients, Detective? I have appointments and responsibilities. I can't just walk out of here because you snap your fingers."

His frown deepened and a muscle twitched along

his jaw. "I'm sorry, but I've already been here for too damn long." He stabbed his finger at her. "You've got two choices, Doctor. Have someone else cover for you or reschedule your patients, but I've been waiting long enough. Either way, you're coming with me."

As though he had cinched a noose around her neck, his statement made the muscles in her throat tighten. She could barely speak.

"Am I under arrest?" she croaked. She should have seen this day coming and consulted with an attorney to find out about her rights.

How could Bryce shift so easily from acting like a human to being a robocop? Why had he bothered to comfort her if his intention was to drag her through the clinic in handcuffs?

His eyebrows rose, as though her question had surprised him. "No, I'm not going to arrest you. There are just too many interruptions here for an interview."

As though to prove his point, the phone on Mari's desk chose that moment to ring. It made her flinch. Out of habit she reached for the receiver, but then she snatched back her hand.

"My voice mail will take a message," she said, and then she bit her lip. What did he care? "Interrogating me would be a big waste of time," she argued forcing the words past the lump in her throat. "As I told you before, I don't know anything about the missing drugs. Why can't you believe me?"

"You may know more than you think." His expression was impossible to read, but then he had always been good at hiding his feelings from her.

What information could she possibly give him that he didn't already have? And how could she convince him, once and for all, of her innocence?

A chill went through her. What if he was lying about not arresting her?

"Should I call my attorney?" she asked, shoving her trembling hands onto her lap so they were hidden by her desk.

He leaned over her, his gray eyes chilling in their intensity. How could she have ever thought his gaze was warm? He was probably searching for some sign of her guilt. "Do you *need* a lawyer?"

Feeling trapped, Mari opened her bottom drawer and took out her purse. She glanced down at the phone as she weighed her options. If she said yes, would that make her look guilty?

"I've got nothing to hide."

"Of course not." His face remained unreadable.

"I need to call and make arrangements from here for someone to cover me." Milla had been supportive, and Mari could count on her to be discreet.

He nodded. "Just say that we need you to come down and give us some background information on Orcadol."

Once again he had managed to surprise her, suggesting a way to lessen her humiliation. She was about to thank him when she recalled that his suspicion was the very reason she needed a cover story.

Wordlessly she had Milla paged, resisting the urge to drum her fingers on the desktop while she waited for the midwife to respond.

"How are Mr. and Mrs. Jenkins doing?" Mari asked when Milla finally came on the line.

"The hospital chaplain is with them now," she replied. "He'll help with the arrangements."

"I'm so glad to hear that." Quickly, Mari outlined what she needed, her gaze on Bryce the whole time. If her scrutiny made him uncomfortable, he didn't let it show.

"Is this because of your friendship with Dr. Phillipe?" Milla asked when Mari was done. "Can't they test him if they don't believe that he's drug-free?"

Ricardo Phillipe was a friend of Mari's who had been connected with early Orcadol development. He was also involved in planning the experimental research facility.

After a car accident in which Ricardo had been critically injured, his wife and small daughter both killed, he had developed a drug problem that led to him losing his license to practice medicine.

Mari swiveled her chair so she was facing the wall. "I'm sure that's not an issue." She lowered her voice even further. "I really can't discuss it now."

"Oh, of course. I'm sorry," Milla replied. "Is there anything else I can do? Can I call someone for you?"

"No, but thanks. I'll talk to you later." Mari knew that Milla was fiercely loyal, but she wasn't so sure about the rest of the staff, not anymore.

And what would her patients think when the news got out that she'd actually been taken downtown for questioning? What about the investors who hadn't already pulled out of the research facility project? Would this ruin any chance she had left of securing the financing to build it?

Lillian Cunningham was the Public Relations director from New York who Mari had recently hired to improve the clinic's reputation. Lily would have a fit when she heard about this! Just because she happened to be in love with Mari's father didn't mean she would cut Mari any slack, either. Lily was one of the best in the business, but she wasn't a miracle worker.

After Mari told Milla goodbye and replaced the receiver, she grabbed her purse and scooted back in her chair, praying her shaky legs would support her.

''I'm ready,'' she told Bryce. What on earth did he think he had on her? His flinty expression told her nothing.

Bryce didn't bother with chitchat on the way to the station that was housed in the Merlyn County Courthouse complex. The fairly new tan building in downtown Binghamton contained all the county's administrative offices.

As soon as he parked in an official space, Mari got out of his sedan without a glance in his direction and marched up the front steps. His legs were longer than hers, so he was able to catch up with her in time to pull open the heavy glass front door.

"Come with me," he said once they were inside. The departments were clearly marked, but he wanted her to lift her head and make eye contact with him.

When she did, she looked as though someone had drained the fight out of her. It was no surprise, after what she'd already been through. She also seemed nervous, again, no big surprise, and—if he was any judge of character—shell-shocked.

Because he knew her to be strong-willed and smart, the last observance startled him. Anyone who managed to successfully complete medical school, an internship and a residency had to be both.

After the conversations he'd had with her over the last few weeks, including their confrontation at the hospital picnic, she must have been prepared for today, unless she wore blinders and went around with her fingers stuck in both ears.

The girl he'd once known very, very well was a lot more savvy than that. Maybe she was merely attempting to play on his sympathies.

There had been a time he would have cut off his hand to spare her the slightest hurt. He had outgrown that kind of foolishness when she ran a spike through his heart and walked away without a backward glance.

He was still plenty attracted to the total package that made up Mari Bingham, even in her loose-fitting scrubs. His reaction to her pissed him off royally. It wasn't his heart he was risking this time around, but his entire law-enforcement career. He'd better get himself focused or he'd wind up back behind the wheel of a patrol car on graveyard shift. Or working as a nighttime security guard for a local warehouse.

Lightly he cupped Mari's elbow. She stiffened, but she didn't pull away. Maybe she was more scared than she let on. Most people were nervous the first time they ended up in this kind of situation and the level of their anxiety had nothing to do with their guilt or innocence.

Wordlessly, he led the way into his home-away-from-home.

"Detective, I've got your messages here," said the civilian receptionist as he approached the counter.

Christine had been hired straight out of high school with an admitted "thing" for cops and their guns. Her jaw worked her ever present wad of gum as she smiled widely and waved several pink slips in the air.

He nodded without breaking stride. She was barely eighteen, but she had already managed to corner him in the break room after shift one evening! Every time he thought about what could have happened if anyone else had come in when he was peeling her off him, he broke into a sweat.

Another phone rang, the new watercooler belched like a scuba diver's tank and the stereo system pumped out classic country. All conversation in the room shut down abruptly the minute its occupants noticed Mari. Just as they had everywhere else in the county, whispers and rumors connecting her with the Orchid black market had been circulating through the department.

Escorting her through the open squad room, Bryce ignored the detective seated at a desk covered with crumbs and candy wrappers, the two uniforms standing by the coffee machine and the one on the phone. In the far corner, a female officer and a teenage girl in camouflage and combat boots had stopped arguing to gawk. As he hustled Mari past Sheriff Remington's office and the storage closet-slash-break room, conversations started up again.

A long-haired creep wearing cuffs leaned against the wall. He skimmed his slimy gaze over Mari, but his knowing smirk vanished when he saw Bryce's glare.

Bryce itched to throw a coat over her, right after he buried his fist in the little prick's ratlike face. Before Bryce could take her into one of the rooms they used for interviews, Hank Butler waved his phone receiver in the air.

"Collins! Got a second?" he called out.

Bryce waved his free hand in response as he pushed open the first door. Whatever Hank wanted could wait.

Except for the requisite scarred table and beat-up chairs brought over from the old building and the two-way mirror on one wall, the interrogation room was as sparse as a cell. No point in making anyone who was brought here feel comfortable.

Mari glanced around. "Charming."

"I wasn't on the decorating committee," Bryce drawled, dragging back one of the chairs. "Have a seat. Want anything? Coffee?"

"I've heard about cop coffee. I'll pass, thank you." She might be nervous, but she held her head high. His father used to say her nose was in the air.

"What, no lie detector?" she asked, turning her head. "No rubber hoses, no holding cell?"

"Someone's already in it," he lied, "but I guess you could share."

She sat down gingerly, as though she expected the chair to collapse beneath her. Folding her hands on her purse, she stared past his shoulder.

She might not want coffee, but he needed a shot of something. Right now the sludge in the bottom of the pot was the strongest liquid available.

"Be right back," he said. It wouldn't hurt to let her cool her heels for a minute, soaking up the atmosphere while he found out what the other detective wanted. Bryce had waited long enough at the clinic.

Leaving the door ajar, he glared at the guy in handcuffs. As he slid his gaze away, Bryce recognized him as a low-level dealer, one who'd probably end up in jail or dead on the street. Guys like this one got busted all the time, but it never seemed to do much good.

Mari stared at the big mirror and tried not to fidget. Someone might be on the other side, observing her behavior and taking notes. Despite her exhaustion, she scraped back the wobbly chair and walked over to the wall, where she very deliberately studied her reflection. She'd watched *Law and Order* often enough to know the setup, but let the detectives think she didn't.

The face staring back at her looked awfully plain, but the lip gloss in her purse seemed too frivolous for the occasion. She limited her primping to tucking some of the loose strands of dark hair behind her ears.

Through the door Bryce had left open, she could hear a couple of male voices. Their conversation sounded guarded, almost secretive, as though they didn't realize they were being overheard. She had enough problems of her own, so she didn't pay much attention to their low-pitched discussion.

It seemed like days since she had lost the poor little neonate, weeks since she'd had a good night's sleep and eons since this cloud of suspicion had first settled over her life.

Feeling slightly dizzy, she sat back down in the hard chair. Where was Bryce? Probably getting even with her.

Let him play his macho games, she thought, smothering a yawn. She would just put her head down for a minute so the room would stop spinning before he came back.

Bryce approached Hank, masking his annoyance. The other detective was overweight and out of shape, with powdered sugar smearing one flabby cheek.

"What did you want?" Bryce asked shortly.

"Got any leads on those vandalized cars out at Ginman's Lake?" Hank asked with an innocent look on his florid face.

"You called me over for this?" Bryce demanded. Everyone in the department knew Hank Butler was lazy. "It's your case, Hank. Why don't you drive out there and ask around? You might learn something."

Scratching the stubble that bristled along his double chin, the older detective leaned back in his chair, gut straining the buttons of his wrinkled shirt. His little pig eyes glanced past Bryce.

"Didn't you and the doc used to date back in the day?" Hank asked, trying to sound cool. "I'll bet you can't wait to get her alone, huh? Work some kind of deal?"

Bryce ignored Hank's baiting. He saw that a greasy-haired lowlife had been brought out of the other interrogation room. He and the other dealer had their heads together while the deputy refilled his coffee mug.

"Why are they here?" Bryce asked a deputy.

The deputy glanced over his shoulder. "Street cleaning," he quipped.

The coffee looked fresh, so Bryce poured two cups. Both of the dealers watched resentfully when he walked past them and shouldered open the door to the smaller room.

"Sorry to be so long," he said, nudging it shut with his foot.

He stopped abruptly when Mari's head popped up from the table. As long as he'd been in the department, this was the first time he could remember having a suspect—especially one who was sober—doze off before an interview.

"You okay?" he asked. She'd been pale before, but now she was as white as the foam cups he was holding. "Need some aspirin?"

She blinked and worked her mouth as though her tongue was stuck. "I'm just peachy, Detective. This has been a red-letter day for me." Her hazel eyes brimmed with resentment. "Could we get on with it, please?"

Here was his chance. Her emotions were high and she was clearly exhausted. She was more likely to slip up and reveal something she would normally have kept hidden, like the truth behind her relationship with Ricardo Phillipe.

Dr. Phillipe had lost his license for illegal drug use. Mari's association with someone having his shady past was too big a coincidence for Bryce to ignore. If he was ever going to solve this case, he needed answers. His professional instincts tugged at him like a bulldog on a short leash.

Carefully, he set her coffee where its aroma would tempt her. Taking the chair across the table, he flipped open his notebook and stared down at his own scribbled handwriting while she blew softly on the steaming cup.

When he looked up, the sight of her sweetly puckered lips made him forget what he was about to say. They stared at each other as color stained her pale cheeks.

"Do you ever wonder what went wrong between us?" The question spilled out before he could stop it.

Her gaze shifted to the mirror behind him. "Detective, is the reason you brought me down here to interrogate me about *my* past? Because if it is, I can assure you that the department will be hearing from my attorney." She scooted back her chair, clutching her purse, and started to rise.

"Please sit down. We're not done," he ordered. Damn, but it hurt that she could dismiss *her* past so easily, as though he had never been a part of it.

She was right about this not being the place to discuss it, even though the room behind the two-way mirror was empty. What had he been thinking?

He ran his finger down the lines on the notebook page, refocusing, and then she made a small sound of distress.

She turned her face away, but not before he saw her eyes fill. The sight of a woman's tears still turned him to putty, especially Mari's tears. He had never wanted to make her cry. How things changed. As he stared, mesmerized by her profile, the only sounds in the room were the ever ringing phone and muted voices from the squad.

Realizing that he had been holding his breath, Bryce closed his notebook with a slap. Perhaps he was getting too soft, but he just couldn't do it. He was determined to unlock the secrets of this case, but if Mari held the key, it wouldn't be today.

"I'll take you home," he said abruptly. "Let's go."

If he had hoped to see gratitude shimmering in her pretty eyes along with the surprise that she quickly masked, he was doomed to disappointment.

"You've wasted my time, Detective, barging into my office and dragging me down here." She got to her feet, head held high. "Next time you'll have to make an appointment like everyone else." Tucking her purse under her arm, she walked out.

Kicking himself for his moment of weakness, Bryce stood in the doorway and watched her leave. He was getting soft, all right. Soft in the head.

She moved quickly, with no sign of the fatigue that had appeared to weigh her down earlier. Had she been conning him? She was already halfway to the reception desk when his frustration spilled out.

"One more thing, Dr. Bingham," he called across the room. "Don't leave town."

When he saw her shoulders stiffen, regret slapped at him like a cold, wet rag. It wasn't Mari's fault that his temperature still spiked whenever he saw her, that he resented the raw lust that surged at inopportune moments or that he hadn't managed to put the memory of losing her behind him.

One thing was as clear as the window to the street. She wasn't about to mistake the drug investigation for some kind of courting ritual, or to jump into the

sack with him for old times' sake. After today he'd
bet she would rather slice him open with a rusty scalpel than look at him, so he needed to get his hormones
under control before he questioned her again.

As Bryce watched her depart, his stomach a tangled
ball of frustration, Hank Butler shoved back his chair
and lumbered to his feet. After he had made a point
to leer at Mari as she disappeared out the door, he
hitched up his wrinkled slacks to the bulge of his gut
and sauntered over to Bryce.

"Gonna visit the doc when she gets sent up?" he
drawled. "After a few months of 24/7 with a bunch
of broads, she might be happy to see you."

Bryce walked away from him without bothering to
reply, but he doubted Hank was right. After this was
over, he'd never look good to Mari Bingham again.

"Where to, lady?"

Mari slumped against the seat of the taxi and gave
the driver her home address. She had planned on returning to the clinic, but she was just too wrung out
to deal with anyone else right now.

As they drove through the downtown area, she
fixed her gaze on the passing scenery in order to keep
her mind carefully blank of the day's events. The cab
passed the white clapboard building that housed the
public library where she had studied with her friends
back in high school, a couple of restaurants she'd
eaten at more times than she could remember, The
Cut 'n Curl, where she had gotten her first perm and

a few bad haircuts, a clothing store and a run-down bar that had both seen better days. Scattered among the familiar downtown businesses were several empty storefronts with For Lease signs in their windows and a few pedestrians on the sidewalks.

If she had been a serious drinker, she might have stopped in at Josie's for a couple of belts before heading home. Even though Mari wasn't on call tonight, the idea of parking her butt on a barstool while she . inhaled secondhand smoke and listened to some boring drunk expound on his political views didn't tempt her in the least.

Gradually the businesses were replaced by small houses. Some were run-down, with dirt yards full of junk and old cars. A few houses were neat and tidy. Children played in the dust or on the sidewalk. Their parents sat in the shade of deep porches and sagging steps. A radio blared. Dogs lazed in the heat. A row of sunflowers added color to the washed-out scene. Oak trees, maples and dogwoods cast long shadows as the sun sank lower in the sky.

The houses got bigger, surrounded by greener lawns, nicer fences and fancier flowers. The cars in the driveways were newer and the trees looked more stately.

Finally the cab driver slowed, turning onto Mari's street. Half a block down, he pulled up in front of a brick building tucked between a white oak and a walnut tree. Four blue doors, one for each two-story condo, were trimmed with identical ornate brass knockers. White shutters framed each window. Matching planter boxes sprouted red and white petunias and dark blue lobelia, and a flag was displayed proudly.

After Mari paid the driver and entered her end unit, she dropped her purse onto the floor of the foyer and sagged with relief against the ivory wall. Lennox, her cat, looked up from the paisley couch where he liked to nap, ignoring his wicker bed.

Jumping down to the carpet with his ringed tail twitching, he meowed a greeting.

"Hey, baby. How was your day?" Mari asked as he rubbed against her leg.

She was about to drop her keys into a pottery bowl on a small table when she remembered that her car was still parked at the clinic. Her hand closed around the key ring and she swung back toward the door.

The quick spin made her feel slightly dizzy. What she needed right now, more than wheels, was something to eat. She'd splurge and call another cab in the morning.

Steadying herself, she bent down to pat Lennox. The gray tabby butted his head against her leg, purring loudly. He looked up with adoring green eyes.

He was the perfect roommate. His love was unconditional. He'd been fixed and—despite having six toes on each white paw—he hadn't yet figured out how to work the TV remote.

When Mari headed for the kitchen, he followed. All she wanted was to toss something frozen into the microwave, pour herself a glass of wine and watch a mindless reality show on television until it was late enough to curl up in bed with her cat and fall asleep.

She filled Lennox's fish-shaped bowl with food, gave him fresh water and nuked her own meal. When it was heated, she sat at her dining-room table, studying the vase of pale yellow roses from her grandmother's garden. They were starting to droop and to lose their petals.

Mari felt pretty droopy herself.

As soon as she was done eating her pasta and shrimp, she disposed of her dish and settled onto the couch with her wine. Her feet were propped on the old trunk that served as a table. Normally the condo was her haven. She had done the decorating herself, using warm, rich tones and filling it with items she loved. Tonight, despite her exhaustion, she couldn't relax.

Ignoring the television, she turned on the stereo. The soothing sound of cool jazz filled the room as she released her hair from its untidy bun and rested her head against the back of the couch. Lennox jumped up and settled onto her lap, rumbling with contentment. Eyes closed, Mari stroked his fur with one hand while she clutched her wineglass with the other.

She sipped her Merlot while she reviewed in her mind every procedure that she had followed in the neonatal unit earlier. It was terribly frustrating that her best hadn't been good enough to save the Jenkins baby.

Until she was able to line up the necessary funding and build her new research center, the more critical cases in Merlyn County would still be at risk. Babies would die and families would grieve.

As Lennox slept peacefully, Mari let her mind shift gears, going from work to the investigation. Maybe she should have insisted on talking to Bryce and getting it over with, instead of fleeing like a rabbit that had been unexpectedly freed from a snare.

Orcadol was a controlled substance, an opiate and a powerful painkiller. In the wrong hands, it could be extremely dangerous. Whoever was stealing it needed to be stopped.

Until now, despite all the signs, it had been hard to convince herself of Bryce's willingness, his obvious determination, to pin the recent thefts of Orcadol on her. After today, she had no choice but to accept that he would. At least she knew that he couldn't possibly have any proof to support his accusation. She was innocent. In time, he would have no choice but to leave her alone and to pursue other leads.

She still didn't understand why he had changed his mind so abruptly today, first holding her in his arms in a clumsy attempt to comfort her and then treating her like a common criminal. Taking her into an interrogation room, but then letting her go without asking a single question about the case. If his plan was to confuse her, it was working!

Mari finished her wine, catching the last drop on her tongue. Once upon a time she had believed Bryce to be a compassionate man—one who would stand by her and believe in her for as long as they lived.

That man, the one she had loved with all her heart, would have known without asking that she wasn't capable of doing anything as heinous as stealing drugs in order to sell them illegally. He wouldn't have doubted her, not even if he had been confronted with a mountain of proof.

She set her empty glass on the trunk she'd found at a flea market, tipped back her head and closed her eyes. She had certainly been wrong about Bryce, drastically so. Could it be possible that right now he was staring at whatever evidence he'd gathered and thinking the same thing—that he had been wrong about her?

As the liquid notes from Kenny G's saxophone faded into silence, the phone rang. It startled Mari and woke the cat, who leaped away like a launched rocket. She let the machine take the call, but when she heard her brother's voice, she grabbed the receiver.

"Geoff! How are you?"

"Right now I'm a little upset," he replied. "Someone I know saw you going into the courthouse with that detective who's been harassing you. I don't figure the two of you were down there applying for a marriage license, Mari, so what gives? And why didn't you call me?"

"I was going to," she fibbed, picturing her brother pacing with his free hand clamped on the back of his neck. He did that when he felt pressured. "I didn't want to interrupt your dinner and irritate Cecilia," she added, trying to placate him. "You're still on your honeymoon."

"Cecilia would understand." He spoke briskly, impatiently. "She knows how important you are to me. Now quit dodging the issue. What happened today?"

Quickly, Mari filled him in on the aborted interview.

"What can I do to help?" he asked. Despite Geoff's many responsibilities at Bingham Enterprises and his recent elopement, he took his family duties seriously. In fact, until he'd met Cecilia, he had always been a bit of a stuffed shirt. Mari didn't know the details, but she knew the other woman had turned his well-ordered life upside down.

"Well, you could give me a ride to the clinic in the morning," Mari replied. "I left my car there this afternoon."

"No problem, but you know that wasn't what I meant when I offered to help." His voice was edged with frustration.

"What did you have in mind?" she teased. "Assaulting an officer? I know you've been trying to loosen up your image, but getting arrested would be a little extreme, don't you think? One felon in the family's enough."

"It won't come to that, sis, but it's time that we hired you an attorney. I know several good ones."

Mari massaged her temple, willing away the headache she could feel coming like a thundercloud building up on the horizon. "I told you before, I don't need an attorney," she said quietly. "I've got nothing to hide."

He released a huff of breath that signaled his impatience. "Hiring an attorney isn't an admission of guilt. You'll need—"

Mari cut him off. "You said that before, but what I need is a ride to work tomorrow. That's all for now, okay?" How could she explain that she just wasn't ready to take that step? Not yet.

From everything she had heard about him, Bryce was a good detective. Despite whatever personal ax he might have to grind, sooner or later he would talk to a witness or uncover new evidence that would make him realize he had been looking in the wrong direction. When that happened, Mari's personal nightmare would be over.

"I'll pick you up in the morning on one condition," Geoff said. He was a skilled negotiator, trained by their father to deal with important clients. Even though Geoff was younger than Mari, when the two of them were growing up he'd always managed to manipulate her into giving him what he wanted.

"What's the condition?" she asked warily.

"Let me line up the best defense attorney I can

find, just in case. You don't have to worry about the bill.''

''That's not the point. I don't need—'' Mari began.

''But your family needs to do something, okay?'' Geoff said. ''Something more than playing taxi while we wait for your detective friend to crack the case.''

She wanted an aspirin. ''Okay.'' Surely this mess would be cleared up soon—any day now—and her life would return to normal.

They set a time for him to pick her up in the morning, she asked that he give his bride her love and they said goodbye. After she hung up and took some aspirin, she turned on the television. Perhaps watching a tribe of ordinary people attempt to outplay, outwit and tearfully eliminate each other on some deserted island would put her own life back into perspective.

Chapter Three

"Collins! Phone call on line two," shouted the uniformed deputy filling in for Christine while she took a break.

Bryce was sitting at his desk with his notes about the Orcadol case spread out before him, but he couldn't concentrate. An hour had passed since Mari stomped out of the office. He might as well leave, too, for all the work he was getting done.

Disgusted with himself for letting her walk away, he picked up the receiver and punched the button that was lit up.

"Detective Collins."

"Hey, bro! How ya doin'?"

His mood dropped another notch. From the giggle that followed Joey's question, Bryce figured that his younger brother was either high or drunk. Unfortunately, Joey had never met an addictive substance he didn't like.

"Hi, Joey. What's new?"

"Oh, not much. Just figured I'd check in with my law-abiding big brother."

Bryce could hear laughter and rap music in the background. Joey seemed to collect no-good bums and losers. No matter how many times Bryce told himself that he wasn't responsible for his brother's behavior, it didn't wash.

"You okay?" he asked reluctantly.

In his opinion, Joey was never okay. The coal mine accident that left their father paralyzed when they were kids had somehow crippled Joey, as well. He had been in and out of juvy for small stuff. Between losing or quitting every job Bryce got him, he'd been arrested for a DUI, shoplifting and possession.

"Right as rain." He giggled again.

"I'm at work, Joey. You must know that, because you called me on the department number. Why didn't you ring my cell phone like I've asked?"

As soon as the words were out, Bryce winced. He hadn't meant to sound so harsh. It wasn't Joey's fault that his own day had gone so badly.

"Sorry, bro. I, uh, I lost your cell number."

"No problem," Bryce replied, struggling for patience. "Let me give it to you again."

He rattled it off and then he made Joey repeat it back. Maybe he'd keep it this time. The way he was headed, he'd probably need Bryce's help.

"I'm about done here," Bryce said. "You want to get a bite? We could go to Melinda's. I'll buy you a steak."

Joey was as gaunt as a greyhound and usually in need of a haircut, but Bryce didn't care how his brother looked. Perhaps he could talk some sense into him.

Melinda's was Binghamton's version of fancy. The decor was a little dramatic, but the food was reliable. On weekends, the live music alternated between country bands and classic rock, but it would be quiet tonight and they could talk.

"Nice of you to ask, bro, but I've kind of got something going here already. Rain check?"

Bryce felt a mix of disappointment and relief that added to his guilt. Where had he failed his only sibling?

"Sure thing. I'll catch you next time."

"One of these days real soon, I'll be the one picking up the check." Joey's voice was hyped. "You wait. Maybe I'll buy you a car, some fancy wheels to replace that piece of crap you drive now."

Joey's bragging barely registered. He always had some deal going, some shortcut to wealth that never amounted to a hill of black-eyed peas.

Once again a corrosive mix of guilt, regret and resentment sloshed around in Bryce's gut like cheap whiskey. "That would be great. Make it red, with a good stereo, okay?"

"You never listen!" Joey's mood flipped abruptly, as it often did. "Don't you p-p-patronize me! I'm gonna show you! I'll show everyone!"

Before Bryce could say anything more, the phone slammed down in his ear. Damn, he thought as tension zinged his brain. Another warm and fuzzy Collins family moment.

He slid open the drawer of his desk, found the battered aspirin bottle clear in the back and shook out two pills. He swallowed them with the rest of his cold coffee. As he shuffled the reports on the Orcadol investigation back into the folder, Hank sidled up to his desk like an overweight crab.

"When you gonna crack the Orchid case?" he asked loudly, jingling the coins in the pocket of his pants. His free hand rested on his gut as if to hold it up. "Got any leads yet?"

Hank's interest was puzzling until Bryce saw that Sheriff Remington's office door sat open.

"Save it, Butler," Bryce replied with a jerk of his thumb. "He's not paying attention."

Hank flushed an unhealthy shade of red.

"You've got the wrong idea," he blustered. "I'm just trying to help out."

A rookie might have been taken in by Hank's innocent expression and his helpful tone, but Bryce had been around long enough to know better. The other detective had a reputation for easing into a case after the legwork had already been done so he could hog part of the credit.

Bryce had already been pointedly rude to Hank today and the other detective still had juice with a couple of old-timers in county government. Hank's other connections were mostly petty criminals and snitches, but antagonizing a fellow cop was never smart. You never knew when you might have to count on him to watch your back.

"I appreciate the offer." Bryce kept his expression bland. "Let me get back to you."

They exchanged phony smiles before Hank lumbered out to the vending machine in the lobby. Just watching him was enough to sink Bryce's mood even further.

Was he seeing a glimpse of his own future? Hank's wife had divorced him years ago and moved away with their daughter. Now he lived alone in a beat-up rental, waiting either for his pension to kick in or a heart attack to drop him—whichever came first. In the meantime, Hank closed enough routine cases to avoid becoming a blip on the sheriff's radar.

"Detective Collins?" As if he had read Bryce's mind, Sheriff Remington stood in the doorway of his office. "Got a minute?"

Bryce blinked and refocused. "Sure thing, Sheriff." He got to his feet and dragged up another smile, one he hoped was convincing. "What can I do for you?"

"Bring the Orcadol file." He went back inside.

Folder in hand, Bryce felt like a kid who'd been summoned to the principal's office. He took the plain wood chair facing the sheriff's desk. Among themselves, the deputies called it The Hot Seat.

"Have you got anything new to tell me?" Remington sat back, his hands steepled and his fingertips grazing his mustache. He gave Bryce his full attention.

"No, sir." Bryce knew from painful experience how pointless it was to jerk his boss around. "I wasn't able to interview Dr. Bingham today like I planned, but I will."

The sheriff's gaze narrowed, but he didn't ask any more questions. Instead he removed a folder from a drawer and slid it across his desk. "This came in a little while ago. It's the analysis on the handwriting recovered from the drug raid."

Bryce itched to open the folder and read the contents. When they'd paid the dealer a surprise visit, they'd confiscated a variety of illegal substances, as well as what looked like torn prescriptions with Mari's name. The signatures were illegible, but the department had ordered a comparison with a sample of her handwriting obtained by its office.

"The handwriting isn't Dr. Bingham's," Remington said. "It wasn't even a good forgery."

Bryce was surprised by the relief that flowed through him. What he should be experiencing was disappointment, since the findings of the report made his case a whole lot tougher.

"I see," he said stupidly.

Remington narrowed his piercing blue eyes. "I've been taking a lot of heat from the mayor's office on this, and I'm damned tired of seeing my name in the *Mage.*"

He was referring to the town newspaper, which had run several editorials questioning the sheriff's priorities. His re-election campaign had included a promise to clean up the county and get illegal drugs off the street, but the arrests they'd made so far hadn't yielded much in the way of either drugs or useful information.

He ran a hand through his white hair. "Last week a reporter from a TV station in Lexington called. She was looking for an interview." Clearly the request hadn't made him happy. "I'm starting to feel like a duck in a shooting gallery, Detective. What's your next move?"

Bryce tapped his finger on the report. "Whoever is responsible for switching Orcadol at the clinic with a different painkiller has got to work there. I'll need access to their personnel records."

The sheriff frowned thoughtfully. "Do you have a plan?"

"I've got an idea that I'm pursuing," he replied, hoping the sheriff didn't ask for details.

The sheriff tapped his fingers on his desktop. "Let's not rule out the doctor yet as a person of interest. She may be connected somehow, since I doubt this is a solo operation. If you lean on her, she may crack.''

"Yes, sir." Bryce picked up the folder. The idea that Mari might have sold or given out illegal prescriptions for Orcadol had never made much sense to him, despite how much his bitter, angry side wanted to believe it. Illegal drug trafficking was a damned risky way to get the money for her research center. Now he was back to square two, looking for the link to the Foster Clinic.

The sheriff reached for his phone. "Keep me informed."

"How are you feeling?" Mari asked Milla as they left the clinic for the day and walked toward the employee parking lot. "Nausea all gone?"

Milla blushed prettily as she glanced up at the man beside her. Mari was sure Milla's high color wasn't just because of the temperature, even though the day was especially warm.

There wasn't a breath of air to stir the tree branches overhead. Even the last of the summer flowers bordering the sidewalk appeared wilted.

"My ankles are a little swollen," Milla confessed. "Other than that, I'm fine."

Milla's fiancé and the father of the baby she was carrying, Kyle Bingham, took her hand in his as he made a point to peer down at her legs in loose-fitting uniform pants and thick-soled white shoes.

"You have the ankles of a gazelle," he told her with a straight face.

Kyle was a resident at the hospital, as well as Mari's cousin. Although Uncle Billy had never gotten around to marrying any of his numerous lady friends, he'd managed to father several children, including Kyle, before perishing in the crash of his plane. Each of Billy's descendants had a different mother. Adding to the confusion, the boy who Kyle was helping Milla raise, named Dylan, was another of Uncle Billy's progeny. Young Dylan was Kyle's half brother.

Despite the dinner that Mari had recently hosted to introduce Kyle into the Bingham family, she hadn't known him well until he'd met Milla. He had done the right thing when Milla got pregnant, but he'd also rescued both her and the clinic in another way.

During a recent home visit, Milla had discovered a new mother dead of a drug overdose and her baby girl in critical condition from ingesting contaminated breast milk. Milla called Kyle and together they managed to save the baby's life.

As fate would have it, the baby's aunt and uncle were the same couple who had filed a malpractice suit against Milla and the clinic for sending their own newborn to intensive care some months ago. When they saw Milla treating their niece, they confronted her.

Kyle overheard the loud exchange and leaped to Milla's defense. He explained to the Canfields that without her quick thinking, the tot wouldn't have survived. He didn't mention his role in the rescue, instead giving Milla full credit. By the time he was through talking, he'd convinced the Canfields that no midwife as caring as Milla deserved to have her career damaged by a lawsuit.

Now she radiated with happiness, despite her swollen ankles and the fact that the day had been a hectic one. Love, Mari thought with a little curl of envy, must do that for some people.

Milla must have read something in Mari's expression, because her smile faded. "This is all so unfair," she exclaimed. "I wish there was something I could do to help the police find out who's really been stealing Orcadol, so they'd leave you alone."

Patting her shoulder, Mari felt the sudden tension. Milla didn't need this kind of stress, not in her condition.

"You've both been wonderful," Mari said. "Milla, I can't tell you enough how much I appreciate everything you did yesterday."

Milla had quietly dealt with Mari's patients after Bryce hauled Mari to the sheriff's office. She had made excuses, rescheduled appointments and fielded questions from other staff members.

"You don't have to keep thanking me," Milla said, clearly embarrassed. "I was honored to help. I could never repay you for all your support."

"I think we're more than even." Mari smiled at Kyle. "Do you realize how lucky you are, cousin?"

With a wide grin of his own, he leaned over to kiss Milla's cheek.

"Absolutely. Having Milla, Dylan and a baby on the way has made me happier than winning the megastate lottery," he replied.

To keep her thoughts from sliding back to her own problems, Mari tried hard to focus on the other couple's obvious joy. Surely someday she, too, would find a man to care about, one who would support her career and help her to finally forget about her first painful love.

Milla's happy smile faded again as she glanced past Mari. "On, no," Milla groaned. "What can he possibly want this time?"

Mari glanced around to see who Milla was talking about. Her entire system jolted when she spotted Bryce leaning against his car, arms folded as he watched them. Despite the muggy heat, he was still wearing a lightweight jacket with his tan slacks, but his folded-up tie was sticking out of his pocket and his shirt was open at the neck. His hair was damp and slightly disheveled, as though he had been raking his fingers through it in the same way he used to do when they studied together. It gave him a youthful air she hadn't seen in a long time, but the gravity of his expression spoiled the effect.

"Would you like me to run him off?" Kyle offered as Bryce approached them.

Mari took a deep breath. How could she find him attractive after everything that had happened between them? She must not have any better sense than a teenage girl with a crush on the boy she knew to be bad news.

Holding tight to her resolve, Mari patted Kyle's arm. "I'll be fine."

She was fed up with Bryce's constant harassment. Yesterday she had been too upset to offer much resistance when he'd hauled her into his arms, but today she was more than ready to vent her frustration.

"You two go on ahead," she told Kyle. "I know you're planning to take Dylan out to dinner. I've got a class tonight, so I'll deal with this little annoyance myself."

"Are you sure?" Milla asked. "You don't have to talk to him. Maybe we should call Lily or an attorney."

Mari shook her head. "I don't need help standing up to a bully." She pitched her voice loud enough for Bryce to hear, but he didn't flinch. Either he'd grown immune to insults or her opinion didn't concern him.

Probably the latter, since he believed her to be a criminal. He had stopped caring about her a long time ago, when she thought they were madly in love and planning a future together. Not only had he spoiled everything by refusing to go with her when she left for college, but he had expected her to give up her dream of attending medical school, so they could both find dead-end jobs here in Binghamton.

"Doctor. Miss Johnson." With a nod, Bryce

stepped off the sidewalk so they could walk by him. Milla returned his greeting softly with her gaze on the ground, but Kyle gave him a level stare.

"Call security if you need any help," Kyle suggested to Mari as Milla tugged on his hand to hurry him along.

"I'm not here to cause problems," Bryce told Mari after the young couple had left. "There's something important that I need to discuss with you privately."

Her resentment bubbled up, nearly choking her as she thrust out her wrists. "Have you come to haul me in again? Well, get it over with."

Wasn't it enough that he had broken her heart and made her forever distrustful of love? Was he determined to ruin the life she had built without him, as well?

Maybe the worst of it was that she still—despite everything—reacted to him more strongly than she ever had to any other man. No one else ever made her feel the way he had.

For years she had managed to avoid him, not always easy in a small town. Being forced to talk to him again, even under these circumstances, was like having a scab ripped away to expose a wound that hadn't completely healed. If he ever figured out how she felt, she would have no choice but to pack up and move away.

When he didn't react to her taunt, she allowed her bare arms to fall back down to her sides. Then she made a show of peering past his solid bulk.

"Where's your backup?" she drawled. "Surely you didn't expect to take down a dangerous felon like me without bringing along a SWAT team in full riot gear." She held up her straw shoulder bag. "Better watch out for the assault rifle in my purse, Detective. And I've got a couple of hand grenades stuffed in my bra."

As soon as the last few words were out of her mouth, she wished she could grab them right back.

His gaze flickered to her breasts in the snug bodice of her red-and-white-striped sundress. When his mouth twitched, she cringed.

"Not a chance," he drawled. "Not if memory serves me correctly."

Her face went hot. Damn him for not being gentleman enough to ignore her comment!

"I wish I *was* armed right now," she hissed, furious. "I'd blast you straight to perdition!"

He didn't react, even though there must be some law against threatening an officer. Instead he looked around, gray eyes narrowed. Some of the people leaving the clinic and the hospital glanced at the two of them with open curiosity.

"Is there somewhere else we can go?" Bryce asked quietly.

Mari's mouth dropped open. Was he serious?

"I don't know about you," she replied, "but I've had a long day." She tried to step around him, but he shifted so that she would have to either walk in the grass or actually brush past his body.

An unwelcome mental image threatened to distract her. When they were in school, Ginman's Lake was where the kids swam and hung out every summer. Of all the boys, Bryce's build had been the most athletic, and all the girls enjoyed sneaking peeks. Did he still work out?

Mari had no intention of finding out, and she wasn't about to get caught up in some bizarre game of dodge and weave while her staff and patients looked on. Clutching her purse, she drew herself up to her full height.

"Let me take you to dinner," he suggested before she could tell him to leave her alone. "Somewhere quiet, so we can talk. There's an Italian place—"

"Have you lost your mind?" she demanded. "Unless you have an arrest warrant in your pocket, I'm not going *anywhere* with you. Besides, I have a class to teach at the elementary school in a little while."

"In case you haven't noticed, school's out for the day," he replied.

"I'm filling in at a parenting class." Too late she realized that she didn't need to explain herself. "I'm in a hurry," she added crossly.

"You won't talk to me, not even to clear your name?" he taunted before she could take two steps away from him.

Just as he'd known it would, the question stopped her in her tracks. Bristling with resentment, she turned back around. How could he tease her about something as important as the professional reputation she treasured?

"You've got thirty seconds to explain that comment and then I'm out of here." Ignoring the rapid thudding of her heart, she folded her arms and tried her best to look bored.

A young intern she recognized from the hospital walked toward them. He must have noticed their angry expressions, because he changed direction abruptly, cutting across the lawn. Everyone, she realized, was avoiding the sidewalk where they'd been standing nose to nose.

The gossip mill would be churning tomorrow!

"It's too damned hot to stand in the sun and try to explain," Bryce replied. "If you don't have time for dinner, we'd better meet here later. When's your class over?"

"Eight o'clock, but the clinic will be closed then." After-hours patients went to the hospital.

He merely lifted an eyebrow.

Silently she searched his face, trying to figure out whether this was just a trick to get her to incriminate herself. He had always been good at hiding anything he didn't want her to see, and nothing had changed. His expression was still impossible to read.

He jammed his hands into the pockets of his slacks, absently jingling his keys. "I don't suppose there's anything I could say to persuade you to trust me, Marigold."

Normally, Mari avoided sarcasm, but his use of her full name was too much.

"Why, I do *trust* you, Bryce," she said, her tone dripping with honey. "I trust you to do everything you can to toss me in the slammer!"

Absently he scratched his jaw while he studied her with a frown. "Okay, I'll tell you something you don't know, a freebie, but you have to keep it to yourself for now."

"Why?" she demanded. What game was he playing?

"What I'm about to say is part of an ongoing investigation," he explained with exaggerated patience. "You can get me in trouble if you're so inclined. Now do I have your word or not?"

Curiosity won out. "Okay," she grumbled.

"You remember we found some of your prescription forms in the possession of a known street dealer." He kept his voice low. "They'd been torn up and most of the pieces were missing, but what we were able to recover had your signature."

"Yes." He'd brought the evidence the last time he'd tried to question her at the clinic.

Bryce raised a finger to his lips. "Don't worry," he said. "We know now they were forged."

"Wait a minute." She struggled to keep her voice even. "What do you mean, we know *now?* Did you really *believe* that I was capable of doing something like that?"

He didn't reply, but the answer was plain.

She took a deep breath as she struggled to steady herself. "Ever since this insanity started and I knew you were investigating it," she said, the words pouring out of her, "I told myself that deep down in your heart, no matter how the evidence looked, that you could never *really* suspect me."

He started to speak, but she held up her hand. "I managed to convince myself that you were trying to punish me for going away to college." Tears filled her eyes. "But I was wrong, wasn't I? You actually believe I'm the kind of person who would steal drugs from my own clinic."

Bryce shook his head slowly, his expression perplexed.

"I'm a cop, Mari. I'm trained to follow the trail of evidence, like a bird dog on a pheasant." He rotated his shoulders as though he was trying to relieve his own tension. "Why is it easier for you to accept my trying to *frame* you than for you to see that including the clinic director as a person of interest isn't completely illogical?" he asked.

Mari blinked away the moisture filming her eyes before it could spill over and make her humiliation complete.

"It's easier for me because the first reason would mean you're a bad cop, but the last tells me you never really knew me at all," she blurted.

He still looked confused. "I'm sorry, but I don't follow your feminine logic," he said finally. "All I got from that explanation is that you don't think much of me as a detective.''

"I don't know what to think anymore," she cried. "What did you mean by that remark about clearing me? Was it just something you said to keep me from walking away?''

He shifted his weight from one foot to the other. "I don't know about you, but I'm damn tired of standing here in the sun debating this.''

Mari knew instinctively that trying to budge him would be futile. Wordlessly, she glanced at her watch. Not only would she not have time to grab a bite before class, but she'd be late if she didn't leave right now. Good thing she didn't have to drive clear out to the high school, ten miles from town.

She dug her keys out of her bag. "Can you meet me in front of the clinic at eight-fifteen?''

Later, while he waited for Mari to show up, Bryce plotted what to say once they got to her office. Derived from opium, Orcadol was highly addictive. In its timed-release form, it was great for pain relief, but drug abusers who chewed or snorted it needed ever increasing doses to get the same high. Without the drug they could become desperate, even violent.

One woman had already died of an overdose, so Bryce felt the pressure to crack this case before tragedy struck again somewhere in Merlyn County. What he had to do now was block out his constant awareness of Mari as a woman, but it wasn't easy.

Relief unclenched the knot of tension in his gut when he finally saw her walking toward him from the parking lot. He'd been afraid she wouldn't show up.

She was still wearing the sleeveless red-and-white-striped dress that reminded him of peppermint candy— sweet and spicy. Her white sandals had thick soles that did nothing to detract from the shapeliness of her legs, and he'd noticed before that her toenails were painted red to match her dress. If he told her that she made his mouth water, she would either slap him or bring him up on charges.

After returning his greeting with a barely perceptible nod, she unlocked the main door of the clinic. He held it open for her to sweep past him with a mumbled thank-you.

After hours, the clinic was totally different than it had been during his last visit. Except for a couple of fixtures left on for security, the only light leaked in through the slats of the window blinds. The building was so quiet that he could hear his own footsteps when he crossed the tiled entry.

She led him into the waiting room where a softly glowing fish tank bubbled in the corner. The toys had been picked up. The magazines and picture books were arranged neatly on the tables. The room looked larger than it had when it was full of patients and their fussy children.

He nearly collided with Mari, who had turned to confront him. Seeing how close they were, she took several steps back.

Too bad if he made her nervous, he thought. He'd offered to take her somewhere less private.

She, too, must have sensed the intimacy between them, because she reached over to switch on a brass table lamp. Its weak glow did nothing to dispel Bryce's awareness of her, so he forced himself to widen the distance between them before he could do something both foolish and unprofessional.

"What do you want?" she asked bluntly.

His gaze drifted to her mouth before he jerked it back up to her hazel eyes. Time was against him. Grimly he focused on his goal.

"We know that someone who works at the clinic is responsible for the Orchid that's been showing upon the street."

"You can't possibly have any proof," she replied.

"I'm trying to help you." He shrugged. "I need your employee records. I'll go through them tonight and bring them back tomorrow."

She was already shaking her head. "That's impossible. Those are private."

"Wouldn't it be better if you'd let me see them and we solve this before there's another victim?" He hesitated before playing his trump card. "Unless you aren't yet ready to give up the spotlight. You must realize that your name is bound to be leaked to the media before much longer."

She glared. "Are you threatening to expose me? I thought the sheriff's department protected people's identities."

"You've got us mixed up with the press. The only sources I protect are witnesses and snitches." He studied her for signs of weakening. "The sheriff is getting a lot of heat from the county council. It wouldn't be the first time a bone was thrown out to give the media something to gnaw on for a little while. You know how it is, big headlines when the news breaks, followed by a tiny retraction later on page ten."

She folded her arms and thrust out her chin in a gesture that jolted him, because he recognized it so well.

"Why are you doing this?" she asked.

Bryce realized his only hope of getting her cooperation was to convince her that he wasn't on some fishing expedition.

"You and I both know the drugs have to be coming from here," he said. "Don't forget the other painkiller that was substituted for the missing Orcadol."

"Switching the medications could have been an accident," she argued.

He stopped his pacing and held her gaze. "Do you really believe that?"

She had taken a little container of mints from the pocket of her dress, just like one he'd noticed the other day. Automatically she offered one to him, but he shook his head. She stared down at her hand for a moment, then tucked the mints back into her pocket without taking one.

"I don't know what to think," she admitted.

"What about the prescriptions we found?" he asked. "How easy would it be for someone from outside to take a few sheets?"

"Not easy at all," she replied, "but I suppose it's possible. I could have left it in an examining room while I went to get something, but that's a pretty big coincidence."

Bryce swallowed his frustration. "How are you going to feel when another patient has an allergic reaction to a pain medication that was supposed to be Orcadol or if a deputy gets shot apprehending an addict who's desperate for a fix, just because you refused to let me follow the only real lead I've got?"

Mari appeared shaken by his question. "That's not fair."

She walked over to the watercooler and filled one of the paper cups. Keeping her back to him, she drank it.

"I imagine that I'd feel the same way you would if someone dies before you find out who's responsible." Her voice was subdued.

Without stopping to think, Bryce walked over and put his hands on her shoulders. When his fingers brushed her bare skin, she trembled. She felt as fragile as a bird and as tense as a trip wire.

He leaned closer. "Then help me," he whispered into her ear.

She bowed her head as he realized what a mistake it had been to touch her. Briefly he allowed his grip to tighten and then he forced himself to let her go.

She didn't turn around until she had put half the room between them. "I can't possibly allow you to take the files out of here. Tell me what you're looking for, and I'll go through the records myself."

He threw up his hands. "I can't draw you a map, Doctor. I won't know what's important until I find it."

He could almost see her regretting her suggestion. In a moment she'd be kicking him out the door with his hands empty.

"There's only one thing left to do," he said, certain he'd live to regret his next comment. "You and I will have to search the records together, even if it takes half the night."

Chapter Four

"Have you found anything yet?" Mari looked up from the employee file she was studying. She was barely able to believe that she and Bryce were snooping through clinic records together for the second evening in a row.

They had barely gotten started last night when she was called away to the hospital for an emergency cesarean on one of her favorite patients. Tonight Bryce had been delayed by a mandatory department meeting. When she asked if it concerned the Orcadol investigation, his reply had been evasive.

Like the Ohio River, information shared between the two of them only seemed to flow in one direction.

Now she sat in her office on the narrow cot she'd used on more than one occasion for late-night naps. Files were spread around her.

Bryce shook his head in reply as he reached for another folder. He was sprawled in her office chair with his legs stretched out in front of him and his jacket draped over the back. His shirtsleeves were rolled up, revealing his tanned forearms.

An hour ago they'd ordered a pizza, half pepperoni and half mushroom, because they were both famished and both had missed lunch. They devoured it with cans of soda from the vending machine and a shared candy bar was dessert.

Pizza-topping preference was one area in which his taste hadn't changed, but she didn't let on that she remembered. Working together in her small cluttered office was difficult enough without reminiscing about their turbulent past.

"How well do you know Marvin Regal?" he asked without looking up. "It says in here that he's only worked at the clinic for eighteen months, but sometimes he's here at night."

"Marvin's a friend of my grandmother's," Mari replied. "He's fallen on hard times, but I doubt he'd be stealing drugs."

Bryce crossed his long legs at the ankles. "What kind of hard times?" He was probably hoping for a felony conviction.

"He bought stock in a company that went bankrupt," she replied. "The CEO made a fortune, but everyone else lost their money."

He wrote something in his notebook.

"Why bother to ask me if you aren't going to listen to my opinion?" she huffed.

When he glanced up, she wondered briefly if it was work or play that made him look a little worn around the edges. She knew he was still single at thirty-six, with a bit of a reputation throughout the county as a ladies' man. Beyond that, she had no idea how he filled his time.

No doubt she must appear equally exhausted. After last night's surgery, her morning had started later than usual with a staff meeting at nine, but two more of her patients were due to deliver at any time.

So far this evening her pager and her cell phone had both been quiet, but she doubted she'd make it through the entire night without another summons. Her busy schedule was her own fault, since she refused to stop practicing in order to run the clinic.

"I'm making a list of everyone who's worked here for less than two years so I can run the names," he replied a little defensively. "Maybe something in their past will pop."

A chuckle slipped out before Mari could prevent it. "Marvin has no criminal record, if that's what you're hoping for. He's an ordained minister who volunteers at the food bank."

"Good cover," Bryce drawled, straight-faced.

She was about to snap back at him when she saw the corner of his mouth twitch.

"He has a three-legged cat he rescued from the shelter," she elaborated. "He brings the clinic staff homemade brownies every Monday and he carries spiders outside in a paper cup instead of letting anyone squash them."

Something sparked in Bryce's cool gray eyes. "I suppose he was an Eagle Scout, too? That he spent his youth helping little old ladies cross the busy streets of Binghamton?"

"I don't know for sure, but there is one big reason not to add him to your hit parade."

Bryce tipped his head, pencil poised. "What's that? He's too honest, too softhearted? Too good a cook?"

"He has no access to the drug cabinet," she pointed out dryly. "Marvin couldn't have switched the pills, so he can't be our thief."

The night before, she had explained who had access to the pharmacy supply cabinet so Bryce could go through those files first. He'd also grilled her in detail about Ricardo Phillipe. After the car accident that had killed his wife and small daughter, he had developed a drug problem, but he'd been clean for over five years.

Was his history the only reason Bryce was still looking at him, or could it have something to do with the fact that she and Ricardo were friends? She must be getting fanciful to think Bryce might resent another man in her life after all this time.

After he had finished reviewing the files for the medical staff, he'd started on those of the office workers, maintenance staff and other support people. The clinic financial records had previously been examined. As far as she knew, nothing questionable had turned up.

With a sigh, Bryce closed his notebook, clasped his hands together and stretched his arms over his head.

"Tired?" she asked.

"Naw. All cops are sleep deprived. It's part of the job description." He cocked one dark eyebrow. "Isn't it the same for baby doctors?"

She almost smiled before remembering that the two of them weren't buddies. "Pretty much."

Slightly rattled by the way he was watching her, she looked back down at the paper in her hand. She'd been skimming a stack of employment applications, searching for anything unusual.

"Get any sleep last night?" he persisted.

"Some." After the C-section, she'd gone home for a few hours, but thinking about the investigation had kept her awake for quite a while.

He cleared his throat. "What are the chances of someone with a key forgetting to lock the drug cabinet and an unauthorized employee getting into it?"

She was about to shake her head, but then she reconsidered. Anything was possible, at least in theory.

"Wouldn't that have to be a crime of random opportunity?" she asked. "Not something that had been planned?"

He shrugged.

"I suppose there's a chance of that happening," she continued, "but as I said before, we have very specific procedures.

"We don't keep a great deal of Orcadol on hand at any one time," she added. "Of course people know it's here because we prescribe it. Some pharmacies don't let anyone know they've got it in stock, not even firefighters and EMTs."

She tucked a strand of hair behind her ear, wishing she'd worn it up as she usually did. Ah, vanity. She had on a long denim skirt and matching sleeveless top instead of the comfortable scrubs she often wore. Not because she was meeting Bryce, of course, but because she had decided to dress up for this morning's meeting.

"I can't rule out anyone who works here at this point," he said stubbornly.

"But how could the cabinet accidentally being left unlocked and someone taking advantage of that cause a flood on the black market?" she asked.

Frowning, he went back to his search. "Yeah, you're right. At best, they might cop a few pills and sell them."

Mari got to her feet. She'd been sitting in one position on the cot, with one leg tucked under her, for too long. Thank goodness they were nearly done.

"You know that you just proved my theory, don't you?" he asked.

Turning away, she bent forward from the waist in

order to stretch out her back muscles. "What's that?" She held one hand against the neckline of her top to prevent it from gaping open—not that she had much cleavage to show off, but she didn't want Bryce getting the wrong idea and thinking she was deliberately flashing him.

"It has to be someone with regular access to the keys who's stealing Orcadol, someone who's had the opportunity to switch it with other painkillers on a regular basis without arousing suspicion," he said without looking up.

Mari had reluctantly reached the same conclusion, but she felt duty bound to defend her co-workers. "I let you look through the files to eliminate my employees from suspicion. You haven't found anything, have you?"

A look of frustration crossed his face. "Not yet." The chair squeaked as he got to his feet. "That doesn't mean it's not in here somewhere."

Mari wasn't sure why she bothered to argue, except that she hated knowing he was probably right. "Maybe you're just plain wrong. First, you accuse my friend Ricardo, just because he's made some bad choices in his life, then you suspect me of stealing from my own clinic and now you're looking at my co-workers, all without any concrete proof!"

"We'll find the proof." His color rose, and he parked his fists on his narrow hips. Obviously he was one cop who doughnuts didn't tempt.

"And you're not off the hook yet, Doctor," he continued. ''Yes, I'm pretty sure it's someone who works here. No, I haven't found anything, in part because no one was about to list anything *incriminating,* like a previous drug conviction, on their employment application. Unless you're lying to me about your security measures, my detective's instinct and my gut are telling me the thief is someone you know and trust.''

Mari shook her head adamantly. ''I already questioned the entire staff. No one knows anything and no one remembered seeing anything suspicious.'' Let him chew on that for a moment.

Bryce leaned down and looked into her eyes. ''What did you expect?'' he asked softly. ''For one of them to confess?''

His condescending tone irritated Mari. True, all she'd learned from her interviews with the staff was that Cecilia was planning her elopement, Crystal missed her little boy while he visited his father in Ohio and Milla was understandably terrified that the Canfield's malpractice lawsuit against both her and the clinic, since dropped, was going to ruin her career as a midwife.

The real reason for Mari's irritation was her growing certainty that one of the staff members she'd questioned had looked her straight in the eye and lied. The idea made her sick because these were all people she cared about. People she trusted.

''Maybe someone got hold of the Orcadol before

it ever got here,'' she felt compelled to point out. ''Have you thought about that, Detective Collins?''

It was his turn to shake his head as he straightened away from her. ''Not likely. The pharmaceutical company's security measures are pretty extensive.''

Mari knew he was right, even though she wasn't about to agree with him.

Bryce raked both hands through his hair, leaving the dark strands sticking up. ''You said before you don't keep much Orcadol on hand, but you go through quite a bit.''

She nodded. ''It's very effective after surgery, as well as for chronic pain. We usually get frequent shipments so we can keep the supply small.''

''Usually?'' he echoed.

He didn't miss a trick, she thought. ''Right now the Orcadol is back ordered, so we've been doling out what we have very carefully so that we don't run out.''

''When's the next shipment coming in?''

She shrugged. ''I'm not sure. The supplier keeps that information confidential.''

''You're the director and you don't know?'' His tone was edged with frustration. Perhaps the confines of her office made him feel crowded, as she did, or maybe he had a girlfriend he was missing.

''I'm a doctor first,'' Mari snapped back at him as she got to her feet. ''Much as you must resent that, even you should realize that I can't keep up on every single detail of the clinic's operation.''

"An Orcadol shipment is hardly a detail." He glared down at her. "What do you mean by accusing me of resenting your career? Just what are you trying to say?"

If she hadn't been so tired, so emotionally drained, so sick at the idea of someone she trusted stealing from her clinic, not to mention her inability to control her attraction to the man in front of her despite *everything,* she would never have given voice to the accusation that had festered in her heart all this time.

"You never wanted me to become a doctor," she blurted without bothering to censor her words. "You did everything you could to discourage me from going to college."

He startled her by grabbing her upper arms and hauling her onto her tiptoes. "You left me in the dust," he blazed. "You never looked back!"

The unfairness of his accusation fueled her anger. "I asked you to come with me! You're the one who chose to stay behind."

His pupils expanded, turning the gray of his irises into thin silver bands. Temper stained his cheeks and his fingers dug into her arms. "Damn it, Mari, I wanted to marry you so that we could make a home together. I wanted a family with you!"

His admission stunned her. She had dreamed of becoming his wife. To hear him say the words now nearly shattered her.

Breathless, she tried to twist away. "You're hurting me."

Immediately he loosened his grip, but he didn't let her go. He had never threatened her, so she wasn't afraid even though she was trembling.

His gaze dropped to her mouth. She didn't want him to know how deeply his confession had affected her, but she was unable to turn away.

A muscle flexed in his cheek as he slid his hands to her shoulders. She could feel the heat radiating from him, could smell his clean scent. She had always loved watching the way his mouth shaped words when he talked. His lips, she remembered with aching clarity, were warm and smooth to the touch.

Did they feel the same? If she lifted her head just a little—

"Mari," he said again on a ragged groan. Awareness flashed in his eyes like silver lightning, and the floor seemed to shift beneath her feet. She needed to step back, to free herself from his grip, to put some distance between them. To remind him, and herself, of why they were here. To resurrect that barrier between them.

Instead she shifted just that tiny bit, her heart racing, her legs shaking, so that only a breath separated her from Bryce.

"Please," she whispered soundlessly.

He didn't hesitate. The touch of his mouth on hers was sweetly familiar and yet thrilling. She froze, and then a burst of heat exploded inside her as he traced a path with his fingers up her throat. Gently he cupped her face in his hands. With his thumbs, he coaxed open her mouth and changed the angle of the kiss.

Wanting more, greedy for it, she yielded to his sweet invasion. She met the thrust of his tongue with her own. Pressing her hands to his wide chest, her fingers curled into the material of his shirt, she felt the heavy thud of his heart under her palm.

He or she, or maybe both of them, moved closer. He slid his hands to her back, gathering her into the circle of his embrace. The small part of her brain that was still capable of thought sent out a jumbled protest. The warning was too little and way too late. Like a candlewick guttering in a pool of heated wax, her resistance flickered and died.

Hunger gobbled her up, flames licking her nerves as he lifted his mouth and then plunged again. Hot and moist. Insistent. Masterful and yet adoring.

He trailed kisses along the line of her jaw, making her tingle right down to her toes. He clasped her hips to hold her close. Desire burned brighter as he returned to her mouth again and again.

She circled her arms around his neck and rubbed herself against him, achingly aware of his arousal. Flattered and captivated. She was both a prisoner of her own passion and a woman who had been set free to revel in it.

Groaning deep in his throat, Bryce lifted his head. When she finally looked at him, his gaze was heavy-lidded, his eyes a swirl of smoke. His cheeks were flushed with passion.

She couldn't let go, not yet. Not after being without him for so long. No other man had ever made her feel as deliciously, wonderfully female as Bryce.

He gave in to the plea in her eyes and kissed her again, devouring her. She feared that her legs would collapse beneath her and she would fall to the floor, so she held him even closer.

His arms tightened and her world spun as he lifted her. She buried her face into his neck, her mouth pressed against his hot skin. She was falling, but she was safe because he had her.

He bent closer, nibbling her throat, and she realized with a blink that he'd laid her on the cot. He braced his arms on either side of her and stared intently as the very air crackled between them. As dangerous as heat lightning.

A lock of his hair had fallen across his forehead, reminding her more than anything of the way he'd looked back in school. Even then he'd been all dark slashing brows and thick lashes that framed the changing shades of his eyes. Maturity had honed his cheekbones and shadowed his jawline, roughing up his looks. And yet the man was even more compelling than the youth had been.

He leaned down and kissed her again, scattering her observations like leaves before a storm. She reached for him. With a moan, she gave herself up to the need and the moment.

Bryce lay sprawled on the carpet, eyes closed, heart still thudding like a kettledrum and his muscles as slack as a dead snake. Like a spark in a haystack, the passion smoldering between him and Mari had erupted into a fireball. There was nothing left of his mind but ashes.

But damn, *damn,* he thought with a groan, she was hot.

He'd barely remembered to slip out of his holster and into protection. Good thing he always carried it with him, no exceptions.

He noticed one of his shirt buttons on the carpet. His pants were around his ankles and she was still half-dressed. While she began silently tugging and straightening, he put himself back together, too.

Time for damage control, he realized. His spirits sank with disappointment when she didn't say anything.

This was all supposed to have been simple, just a kiss to break the tension building between them.

Already the situation was complicated. He wasn't a man to duck away from the truth, but he hated admitting, even to himself, how much he had missed her.

Damn. He scrubbed a hand over his face, wondering how *she* felt about what had just happened. She had practically begged him to kiss her and he had dived right in. She hadn't hesitated except to tell him to shut the damned door to her office while she closed the window blinds.

"You okay?" he asked.

Head bent, she buttoned her top. "Uh-huh. You?"

The distance in her voice snapped his good intentions like a dead twig.

"Mari, look at me." His tone was what he'd use on a green recruit. Damn, but he was doing this all wrong, even though he couldn't seem to stop himself from making it worse.

"I didn't exactly jump you." Real smooth, Collins. When in doubt, get defensive.

She stared at him with a brittle smile. "Afraid I might cry 'police brutality'?" she taunted.

His heart jammed right up into his throat. He hadn't been thinking, just following his…not his brain, that was for sure.

"Oh, don't worry," she chided. "I'd say that we pretty much jumped each other."

The relief he felt was like realizing the bullet fired straight at him had missed. He leaned over to run a path down her cheek with one finger.

"You're almost too much woman for me, sweetheart. I'm surprised the walls are still standing."

She shrugged, her gaze unreadable. "They were built to last."

Did she mean *unlike us?* He didn't want to ask, *are you sorry for what we did?* What if she said yes?

Silently they finished dressing. He couldn't remember kicking off his shoes, but he found one under her desk. She stood up and twisted her skirt around so it hung straight. He adjusted his holster. It was amazing that they'd both fit onto the short, narrow cot, but they hadn't exactly been lying side by side.

She must have noticed the direction of his gaze. "Doesn't look wide enough, does it?" she asked.

"It wasn't." He touched her hair with his hand. "I meant what I said, Mari. You burned me up." He had to stop to clear his throat, and then he lifted her chin with his finger.

Her eyes widened when he leaned down and kissed her, as gently as he knew how. To his surprise, she pulled away.

"This shouldn't have happened, not with the investigation and all," she said, voice husky.

"One has nothing to do with the other," he replied, stomach knotting. "You didn't think you *had* to, uh, to be with me, did you?" He stabbed his hand in the direction of the cot. "That I might—?"

It was Mari's turn to reach for him. She grabbed his arm. "No! No, of course not."

The knot in his gut loosened slightly when he hugged her. "Good," he whispered into her hair. "We'll keep it separate from everything else, I promise."

"What do you mean?" She jerked out of his embrace. "What are you saying, Bryce?"

"Now that we've found each other again, I don't want to just up and call a halt," he admitted.

She turned away from the intensity of his gaze to fiddle with the window blinds. When she slanted them open, the outside lights glowed softly. Except for the moths dancing around each bulb, this side of the medical complex was quiet. "We'd be crazy to continue."

"We'd be crazy not to," he argued.

Ignoring his comment, Mari couldn't do anything except keep staring out the window. Her heart warred with the instinct that was screaming at her, telling her she would be a fool on so many levels to let temptation cloud her judgment. Especially now, when she had so much to lose.

"What are you thinking, Marigold?" The years had deepened his voice. Right now it was a sexy growl that stirred an immediate response deep inside her.

What had she done?

"Some days I work twenty hours," she exclaimed as she turned to look at him. "The investigation has dragged on for weeks, along with the gossip and the suspicion!" She glanced meaningfully at the rumpled cot. "I can't take on anything else."

Lacing her fingers together in front of her, she searched his face. "I'm sorry. I didn't mean to make you sound like just another problem."

He raked a hand through his hair and began to pace the confines of the small room.

"Do you think the timing is any better for me?" he demanded. "I'll agree that it isn't the greatest, but sometimes we don't get a say in that." He stopped in front of her, arms at his sides. "Let's not make any big decisions right now," he pleaded softly. "I know you wouldn't be here with me if you were seeing anyone else, so let's just watch what happens."

His words sent a blush to her cheeks, but before she could comment, he rushed on. "I haven't dated anyone for months. We're both free, and we're in this other thing together. It's late, and we're both tired. Put it on hold, okay?"

Mari glanced at the wall clock. She had to be up early. No doubt, so did he. She didn't feel like arguing anymore tonight.

"I need to know one thing," she asked. "Do you still suspect me of stealing Orcadol?"

"The evidence is inconclusive," he replied, frowning thoughtfully, "so I guess that I couldn't really rule you out at this point."

Mari gaped at him. What she needed was a heartfelt denial, not a professional opinion. Her expression must have shown him that he'd made a tactical error.

"No, hey," he said, opening his arms. "I'm sorry. You caught me off guard. I was thinking like a cop."

She realized that neither of them was going to be able to put the case aside for a few more rounds of slap and tickle.

"I think you've made your opinion crystal clear." Her voice was ice-cold. "Obviously your standards are pretty darned low in some areas, *Detective*."

She would *not* cry!

"Damn it, Mari. You know that's not what I meant."

"No," she protested, shaking her head. "I don't

know anything about you, not anymore.'' Pain and anger swirled together, stealing her breath as she backed away.

To her surprise, Bryce followed. "Then know this.'' His voice shook with intensity. "I want you. Whatever else happens, as of right now we're in this thing together.''

Before she had a chance to think, to ask what he meant, to say anything, he lowered his head. Resistance to the passion that flared up instantly was impossible. Helplessly, she surrendered. As she did, he groaned and broke away.

"Son of a—'' he exclaimed, exasperated. "My pager's going off.''

Chapter Five

Mari spent the next two days avoiding Bryce. Until she could figure out her own reaction to what had happened between them, she sure as heck wasn't ready to deal with his.

Thanks to a full schedule of appointments and meetings, she managed to stay busy. Not thinking about him, not remembering how he had made her feel, was harder, but she tried.

The hospital auxiliary hosted a going-away party in the afternoon for the director, Eric Mendoza. Mari's emotions were mixed when she made an appearance.

Born into poverty, Eric had worked his way up to

his position at the hospital. In a time when many medical facilities were drowning in red ink and staffing problems, he had not only maintained Merlyn County Regional as a level-three trauma center, he had expanded it.

On more than one occasion, he and Mari had worked together. Sometimes they disagreed, but she respected him. Recently he had accepted a position with Bingham Enterprises, which was a wonderful opportunity for him.

Eric's recent bride, Hannah, attended the party with him. As she stood at his side, her blond hair was a perfect foil to his Latin coloring. It was easy to see that he was besotted with her, as he was with the tiny baby girl who slept through the festivities in her carrier. Hannah was another of Mari's cousins by her late Uncle Billy.

Eric's sister, Cecilia, had recently become Mari's sister-in-law when she eloped with Geoff. Since Cecilia worked as a nurse-midwife at the clinic, she was at Eric's party, too.

"Geoff says to stand tall," Cecilia whispered, coming over to give Mari a supportive hug after the cake had been cut. "We're both proud of you."

"Thanks, honey. How's Geoff?" Mari asked.

"He went to Atlanta on business, but he'll be back tomorrow. We're going to the cabin for a couple of days."

"That sounds heavenly," Mari said on a sigh.

"You're welcome any time," Cecilia replied. "How about this weekend? Can you get away?"

"Thanks for the offer, but I'd better take a rain check." As tempting as it was, she had too many other things going on right now.

"Hey, Ceece!" called a young nurse, just as one of Mari's grandmother's cronies from the auxiliary approached. With another hug, Cecilia excused herself.

As soon as the party started breaking up, Mari said her goodbyes and slipped away. She stopped by her condo just long enough to feed Lennox and check her phone messages.

She still hadn't heard from Bryce, not since he'd been called from their heated tryst in her office by an urgent page. She kept telling herself she was relieved by his silence, even if it meant that he didn't have any new information to report.

Grabbing the overnight bag she'd packed that morning, she left to attend a conference at The University of Kentucky. Lexington was a pleasant two-hour drive away.

After checking into her hotel, she changed into a dressy midnight-blue pantsuit for a reception at the UK Medical Center. She was in search of potential investors to replace the ones who had lost interest in funding her research facility. The wealthy couple she had hoped to meet at the reception didn't show up, but the evening served as a distraction from Mari's other concerns. By the time she fell into bed later, lulled by a glass of excellent Merlot and a gentle breeze through the open hotel window, sleep came quickly.

The Prenatal Genetics Conference at UK opened in the morning with a breakfast and roundtable discussion on stem-cell research. It was followed by a full day of presentations, including one on percutaneous umbilical blood samplings and another dealing with blood testing for chorionic villi. The luncheon speaker was a board-certified geneticist whose work Mari especially admired and the afternoon was taken up with demonstrations.

Despite the busy schedule, her mind kept returning to Bryce. Every time she recalled the dark glitter of his eyes and the husky catch in his voice when he kissed her, she felt a shiver of desire that was nearly impossible to ignore.

She should have kept her distance!

Since a trusted neighbor was feeding Lennox for her, Mari had planned on staying in Lexington for a second night to attend an evening performance by the philharmonic. She wanted to visit the Children's Museum in the morning before meeting an old friend from medical school for lunch.

Bryce finally got around to leaving a couple of messages on her cell, but she ignored them. She wanted to see him when they talked, so she could watch his face and try to read him. One moment she was eager to speak with him and the next she dreaded it.

She couldn't be homesick already and she refused to miss him, but the longing to leave kept growing. During the last program about a promising new type of in vitro monitor, she couldn't stay focused.

She was wasting her time in Lexington. She gave away her symphony ticket, canceled lunch with her friend and checked out of the hotel.

"I ain't heard nothin' about Orchid, man. I can't tell you what I don't know." The addict and sometimes paid informant hunched his skinny shoulders. His gaze slid away from Bryce's as the two of them sat side by side on the loading dock.

After running down leads that turned into dead ends all afternoon, Bryce had spotted Morel behind a deserted warehouse. Now Morel watched the empty street as though he expected something to jump out of the shadows. Nothing stirred, not even a breeze to move the sticky heat.

Sweat beaded his lip and ran down the sides of his face. His fingers, their nails encrusted with grime, plucked nervously at the hole in the knee of his worn, stained pants.

"What's got you so nervous?" Bryce asked, struggling to control his impatience as he lit a smoke and held it out. A cold beer would sure taste good right now.

Hell's bells, he was getting soft.

The informant nearly dropped the cigarette. "Just trying to survive," he muttered after he'd taken a long drag and coughed up half a lung. "It's tough out here, you know?"

Bryce shoved his sunglasses back up his nose. "Say the word and I'll get you into a rehab program."

Once upon a time, Morel had been a productive member of society, before a water-skiing accident introduced him to the use of opiates to deal with the pain of a twisted knee.

He was still in pain, his life a mess. Perhaps someday he would get the help he needed, but today he was just one more contact who wasn't talking.

"I'm not ready for that." Morel wet his lips with little lizardlike flicks of his tongue before taking another drag and pushing out two long streams of smoke.

Bryce shrugged. The air was so thick and heavy that even breathing took an effort. Talking was almost too much trouble.

"I'll keep my ears open, though. How's that?" Morel's expression pleaded, like that of a mistreated dog hoping desperately for the treat he knew wasn't coming. He eyed the bills in Bryce's hand and licked his lips again.

"I'll keep my money till you've got something for me." Making a show out of folding up the bills, Bryce shoved them back into his pocket.

He knew that whatever Morel got paid went up his nose or into the rail-thin arm poking out from the sleeve of his sweat-stained shirt. The jacket Bryce had brought him last time was already lost or stolen. Or more likely, bartered for a few pills.

Morel ran a trembling hand through his thinning, greasy hair. "How 'bout a down payment?" he begged. "You know I'm good for it. I'll ask around. I can bring you something real soon, I promise."

Bryce wanted to slap away the mosquito whine of the informant's voice. Instead he leaned closer to Morel, ignoring the ripe odor.

"What I know," Bryce said in a low voice, "is that someone's putting a lot of O on the street. You get me something and then we'll talk."

Bryce could tell that he was wasting his time. He hopped down to the ground and walked away, shutting his ears to the other man's empty promises. Drugs might work miracles for some, but on the street, they twisted lives like knots on a rope.

Hell. Usually Morel would betray his grandmother for drug money. It was odd he had no information to sell today. Either he didn't know or he was too scared to talk.

The danger barometer in the middle of Bryce's back, the one between his shoulder blades, started itching as he walked back to his car. Three guys playing dice in a doorway watched him without speaking. An old man pushed a cart filled with trash, one wheel lurching like a drunk. Two girls on the corner ignored them all, giggling and chewing gum while they watched for cars.

Senses alert, Bryce checked his tires for damage

before he slid behind the wheel and cranked up the air-conditioning.

He could have boiled an egg in the water bottle on the floor. Even as the sun danced along the ridge of mountains, looking scenic, the heat dried him out like a strip of beef jerky.

He had wasted the day, killing time until Mari decided to come home from Lexington. Like Morel, waiting for a fix with his tongue hanging out, Bryce couldn't wait to see her.

He checked his phone, but she hadn't called. He'd held back on contacting her so she would have time to miss him. Then he finally cracked, only to learn that she was out of town.

He'd like to haul her butt right down to the jailhouse the minute she got back, just for making him mad. For making him wait, because she could. For messing with him, because he'd allowed it.

Powerless to stop the surge of heat threatening to sear his common sense, just thinking of her lying on that cot, he gritted his teeth against the rush and thumped his forehead on the steering wheel.

"Hey, honey, want to party?" The knock on the car window made him jump, biting his tongue.

The girl staring at him through the glass was as tempting as stale coffee, despite a pouty mouth and a plunging neckline. If she'd been armed, she could have blown his head off.

Reluctantly he rolled down his window. She looked so damned young.

"Hey, darlin, what's happening?" he asked. As heat and the scent of cheap cologne poured into the car, he went back to work.

During the drive home, stretched out longer by the exodus of traffic from the city, Mari listened to Sting and let her mind wander. She passed sprawling estates and breeding farms, rolling hills and long, low buildings.

She had grown up with a girl's typical love for horses, especially the elegant Thoroughbreds for which her state was famous. Today the pastures might as well be filled with crude plaster statues for all the notice Mari gave them. Her gaze stayed riveted on the road ahead, but her thoughts wandered like geese in the park.

Since her breakup with Bryce, she'd had a couple of intimate relationships. In college she'd had a rebound affair with a jock, followed by a pleasant but ultimately unsatisfying association with a colleague at the local hospital.

It ended when Jay began talking marriage, and she realized that everything about him bored her. To her relief, he accepted a post in Seattle, sparing her any awkward encounters at work. For a while, after he left, it seemed someone was always trying to fix her up, but she'd become adept at making excuses until all but a couple of die-hard family members had lost interest in finding Mari a mate.

She swerved the car around a pair of bicyclists in

helmets and tight shorts, peddling furiously. Glancing in her mirror, Mari cut back over.

She tried to be careful and courteous, a person whose every choice was a cautious one. Never before had she tumbled into the sack as quickly, as impetuously or with such enthusiastic hunger as she had with Bryce. Nor had she ever experienced such complete and shattering fulfillment in anyone else's arms.

Just remembering the way he had made her feel sent a ribbon of fresh desire spiraling through her. She groaned softly and her grip tightened on the steering wheel. Despite the concerns dogging her for weeks, she felt a sudden rush of energy that made her glad to be alive.

With a toss of her head, she cranked up a Rod Stewart classic on the CD player and belted out the lyrics right along with his ravaged voice. She'd been too busy to miss the physical side of romance until, like the prince in the fairy tale, Bryce had reawakened her with a kiss.

Outside the delivery room, she liked order and routine. Everything connected with Bryce was beyond her control, first the investigation and the growing rumors, then the suspicion pointed her way and the disappearance of investors and now this…hunger burning inside.

She felt like a biker peddling helplessly as he raced toward a crash. Perhaps, instead of analyzing it to death, she needed to jump in and enjoy the situation while it lasted.

As quickly as it had risen, her mood plummeted.

Unless she and Bryce sat down and figured out what had gone wrong in the past, which wasn't going to happen in this lifetime, she might as well forget about any chance for a future together. Indulging in no-strings passion had solved nothing. For her, at least, it had only complicated the situation further.

Passing another large horse farm, she glanced out the car window to distract herself. Through a wrought-iron gate set in creek stone, she could see a long driveway lined with blue-and-white flowers and two rows of trees. At the far end sat a stately red-brick house on a slight rise. To one side was a cluster of other buildings, including a matching stable topped with a weather vane. Near it was a covered riding arena. Surrounding the structures were pastures dotted with grazing horses. The scene was idyllic, a counterpoint to her own life.

Closer to home, she stopped at a roadside café for a glass of iced tea and a seafood salad, most of which she left on her plate. By the time she pulled into her assigned parking spot at her condo, she'd reviewed in her mind all the reasons why getting involved with Bryce, even temporarily, was a terrible idea.

A blooming bush nearby perfumed the warm night air when she got out of the car. An overhead fixture made a circle of light, surrounded by darkness. The neighborhood was relatively safe, but she wasted no time retrieving her overnight bag from the trunk.

Before she could straighten back up, a movement

at the edge of her vision stopped her breath. Fumbling with the pepper spray on her key ring, she whirled around, arm extended, just as Bryce stepped from the shadows with his hands palm up.

"Mari, whoa, it's me!" he exclaimed, raising them higher. "Jeez, I didn't mean to scare you."

Heart in her throat, she fell back against the fender of the car. "Are you nuts?" She waved the small canister at him. "If this was a gun, I might have shot you."

Slowly he lowered his hands and shoved them into the pockets of his slacks. "Well, that would be embarrassing for both of us, wouldn't it?" he drawled.

"For you, maybe," she replied.

His expression was unrepentant. "Mind lowering your weapon there 'fore it goes off, little lady?"

Taking refuge in anger, she grabbed her bag and closed the trunk with a slam.

"What do you want, John Wayne?" she demanded. "I need to go inside and feed my cat."

"I called your cell," he countered. "Why didn't you answer?"

She wished she had. Then maybe he wouldn't be standing in front of her now, six solid feet of attractive male. He was unshaven, but the dark stubble made him look deliciously dangerous.

She ignored his question. "Are you sure you weren't worried that I'd try to slip out of the country after you ordered me to stay put? Doesn't the sheriff's department brag about never losing their man?"

"Uh, I think you've got us mixed up with *Sergeant Preston of the Yukon,*" he replied, looking her over in a way that made her blush. "I don't suppose I need to mention that you don't look like any man I've ever been after." His voice dropped to a whisper. "Even with your clothes on," he added.

"Funny," she drawled. "I happened to be at a medical conference on prenatal genetics at UK."

"Fascinating, I'm sure. One of these days you can tell me all about it. Then I'll recite for you the chapter on the basics of crime-scene evaluation from the police-academy training manual." His tone was dry, but his gaze made her feel as though he'd stripped off the wrinkled shorts and blouse she'd been wearing for the last few hours.

"I can hardly wait."

He reached for her overnight bag, but she tightened her grip and shook her head. "Me, too. We can do it nude," he replied. "See anyone special at your *seminar,* Doctor?"

His question surprised her into answering. "Just a few colleagues and a couple of old friends from medical school. No drug connections, though."

She probably shouldn't have added that last bit.

"Would have made my job a hell of a lot simpler if you had," he grumbled.

Her mouth fell open. "Am I being tailed?" The idea hadn't occurred to her until this minute.

"Hell, no. Our budget isn't big enough to follow you all over the state."

She studied him for a moment. He looked tired and cranky, exactly the way she felt.

"Any new leads?" she asked.

"Sorry, no. Miss me?"

"Sorry, no," she echoed.

He leaned against the light post. "Don't you want to know whether I missed *you?*" The corner of his mouth twitched as if he was inviting her to share a joke, but his eyes stayed serious.

Annoyed by the jolt of unwelcome attraction, she brushed past him. "I never ask a question if the answer doesn't interest me."

Braced for a searing retort, she refused to hurry. The silence behind her lifted the hairs on her neck. Had he left?

Suddenly his hands gripped her shoulders, making her yelp in surprise as he spun her around to face him. Her overnight bag landed on the sidewalk next to her feet with a soft plop.

"What?" she squeaked, staring into his glowering face.

"I've spent two long days wondering what you were doing," he whispered harshly. "I'd say that you owe me this much."

Before she could protest that she owed him nothing, he covered her mouth in a kiss nearly punishing in its intensity. Reaction shot right down to her toes, blistering every nerve along the way. The immediate heat between them melted her shock. Her response to the kiss left them both trembling and gasping for air when they finally broke apart.

It was only then, heart thundering, lips tingling, that she remembered her earlier resolution not to indulge herself this way again.

Right now, staring into eyes gone dark with passion, she felt her resolve slipping away. As long as she didn't let her feelings get involved, she bargained silently, she'd be fine. The minute she started falling for him, she'd break it off. That was a promise she made herself.

With his arm around her shoulders, he glanced past her at her condo. "Going to invite me in, sweetheart?"

The familiar nickname sent fresh longing surging through her, reminding her what a dangerous game she was playing. What had she been thinking, to return his kiss with such open hunger?

"I don't think that's a good idea. It's been a long day and the traffic was awful," she babbled. "I have to get up early."

"Tomorrow's Friday," he reminded her softly. "You're not expected back yet, so your schedule is clear. I checked." His gaze narrowed wolfishly. "And I think inviting me in would be an excellent idea."

She could have said she planned to catch up on her administrative paperwork, a necessary task she detested, or she could have come up with a dozen excuses.

"Why?" she asked instead.

He let her go to shove his hands into the pockets of his slacks. "Maybe you don't care what your neighbors might see if we stay out here," he replied, glancing at the nearby buildings. "Rumors about us making out in the parking lot would probably boost my reputation a hell of a lot more than yours." He shrugged, moving closer. "Whatever you prefer."

His grin was so darned attractive that she could have slugged him, just on principle.

"We need to talk," she said gravely.

"My point exactly." With a mocking bow, he picked up the tote she had dropped when he kissed her. "Lead the way."

Beneath Bryce's calm exterior he was a simmering mass of male frustration and uncertainty, ready to boil over like an unwatched pot of burgoo, the local specialty. Her kiss had certainly told him the last couple of days had been as long for her as for him, but he had never been able to read her with any real certainty. All he knew was that she had left him once before, battered and aching. This time he wasn't letting her go until the fire in his gut was thoroughly doused with no live embers remaining.

He'd driven by her condo once or twice, but of course he'd never been inside. The building looked like a palace compared to the duplex he rented across town. He'd moved there after his last girlfriend started pushing for marriage.

Without speaking or looking at him again, Mari unlocked the front door, switched on the light and led him inside. He wanted her so badly that holding off made him shake, but he figured glancing around first was the polite thing to do.

"Nice place," he said, surprised that what he saw wasn't froufrou or flowery.

"Thank you." She seemed a little hesitant. It couldn't be nerves, not after the way they had gone at each other before.

Unless she was having second thoughts. The idea sent a chill sliding down his spine like ice.

"Come in and sit down," she invited when he remained standing in the entryway. "Would you like something cold to drink? Or I could make coffee. It will only take a moment."

Before he could refuse, her cell phone rang from inside her purse.

"Ignore it," he said quickly. "You aren't on call tonight. You aren't even in town."

She frowned at him as she opened her bag. "I still have patients who may need me."

"Then what's the point in having a weekend off?" he demanded, unable to hide his mounting impatience.

Ignoring him, she checked her phone. "It's my service," she said coolly. "Excuse me."

Frustration rising, he wandered into the living room before he could make things worse. A gray cat sat on the couch, watching him silently.

It figured that Mari liked cats. Bryce was a dog person, even though he worked too many hours to have one right now. Leaving it alone so much wouldn't be fair.

It was different with cats, though. They just lay around and slept all the time. Probably didn't know if anyone was home or not and didn't care either way.

This cat hadn't moved, so he approached it slowly with his palm out. "Nice kitty."

It probably slept on Mari's bed. He didn't want it pouncing, claws extended, onto his bare back at an inopportune moment, so he'd better make friends.

The feline stare was unblinking, like green glass, as Mari walked briskly into the room.

"I see you and Lennox have met."

The cat lost interest in Bryce, hopping silently to the carpet and going straight for her. As she bent to pat Lennox's striped head, he wound himself around her ankles.

Well, Bryce didn't blame him. She had great legs, especially in the shorts she was currently wearing.

"What's wrong with its feet?" he asked. "Looks like it's wearing mittens."

She gave the cat's head a final pat and straightened up. "He's got extra toes, six on each paw."

Bryce attempted to appear fascinated. "Huh," he said, staring at the fat white feet. "Has he been de-clawed?"

"I'll let you find that out for yourself," Mari said, "but right now you'll have to leave."

Lennox walked out of the room with his ringed tail straight in the air, meowing insistently. Bryce thought she'd been talking to the cat, but then he realized she was looking at him expectantly.

"Why?" he asked. Even to his own ears, his voice bordered on petulant. "I thought you wanted to talk."

Great. Now he was whining. In a moment he'd be on his knees, slobbering like a Saint Bernard. Not quite the image he was going for.

"That was the hospital calling to tell me that one of my patients has gone into premature labor." She appeared distracted, her mind already elsewhere. "It's Lori's first pregnancy and she's a little nervous, so I have to go."

Bryce had stopped thinking with his brain the moment he'd watched her extend one long leg, bare to midthigh, when she got out of her car. His blood supply had left his head to settle elsewhere.

"With a schedule like this, how do you expect to have a life?" he grumbled, regretting the words as soon as they left his mouth.

"You can ask me that, considering *your* job, Sergeant Preston?" She dropped her cell phone back into her bag and scooped her keys from a pottery bowl on the table. "At least no one shoots at me when I'm working!"

"I'm not a deputy in a patrol car," he protested, stung by her comment. "I'm usually investigating cases, not getting caught in a cross fire!"

She rolled her eyes. "Whatever."

"Also, unlike you, I usually work a normal shift."

"Hah!" She waved a finger under his nose. "You worked pretty late on employee records the other night."

"That wasn't all work, if you recall," he drawled, feeling smug when color painted her cheeks. "At least I have a life away from the job."

Not true, a little voice in his head complained. The closest he'd been to a date in months was getting propositioned by a working girl when he was on loan to vice.

The statement was barely out of his mouth when his own phone rang. Swearing under his breath, he checked the display. What rotten timing.

"It's my boss," he muttered. "I have to take this."

"You were saying something about having a life?" Mari taunted as he turned his back.

The moment he ended the call, she herded him outside. "Was that about the stolen Orcadol?" she asked as she locked the door behind them.

He thought about ramming his fist into the brick entry wall to redirect his frustration. "I can't discuss it," he replied instead, not about to admit that he'd been called because the mayor's car was missing.

It was still early in the evening when Mari finished checking on her patient, who wasn't dilated and whose labor had stopped. Mari should have been exhausted from the long day. Instead she felt restless, unready to face her empty condo.

"Hey, Doc, a few of us are going to Josie's for a cold one. Want to come along?" asked a surgical tech as he held open the front door for her with a glance at her bare legs.

She wasn't in the mood for loud music and secondhand smoke, nor was she dressed for it in the same shorts and top she been wearing since she left Lexington hours earlier.

Before she could answer, another voice spoke from behind her. "I was just about to invite you out for coffee."

"Ricardo!" Mari exclaimed, turning to smile up at her friend and colleague. "How have you been?"

"Am I interfering with your plans?" he asked Josh politely.

"Could I have a rain check?" she suggested to him. "It's been a long day."

"Sure, Doc." The tech flashed a dimple. "Catch up with you later."

"Oh, to be that young again," Ricardo murmured, watching Josh break into a trot.

"And that energetic after a double shift," Mari added. The tech had a reputation with the nurses and midwifery students, one she suspected was well earned.

She turned back to Dr. Phillipe. "Thanks for rescuing me," she said. "Is the offer of coffee still open?"

When he smiled, his entire face brightened. "Of course. There's a new diner in South Junction, right on the way to the middle school. It stays open late. Have you been there yet?''

Mari shook her head. "I've been too busy staying out of jail."

Ricardo's eyes widened. "Has it really come to that?''

"I'll fill you in when we get to the diner," she replied. "Shall I follow you?''

"My car's right over there, if you want to ride with me.''

"Thanks. What's the name of this place," she asked as they walked together down the sidewalk. He was a trusted friend, strictly platonic, but a good listener.

"It's called The Buttercup. They serve fresh pie that the owner's wife bakes in the back.''

He opened Mari's door before going around to the driver's side. She sank into the soft leather seat as he started the engine. Classical music played softly.

By unspoken consent, they didn't talk about the missing Orcadol until after they were seated in a yellow-and-white checkered booth at the diner. Mari was happy that no one else was close enough to overhear them as long as they kept their voices down.

"How are you, really?" Ricardo asked after the waitress took their orders. His expression made Mari regret her quip about staying out of jail.

"I just learned that the case against me had a setback," she admitted, wanting to reassure him.

His dark eyebrows lifted and he leaned closer. "Oh?"

Too late she wondered if it was okay for her to discuss what Bryce had told her, especially with someone she knew the sheriff's department had looked at closely. Well, she couldn't very well back up now. She trusted Ricardo, even if Detective Collins didn't.

Mari waited while the waitress poured two mugs of coffee. "Pie's coming right up," she told Ricardo with a smile. "You wanted the peach, right? Heated, with ice cream?"

He nodded. "Please."

After she'd left without a glance at Mari, he smiled teasingly. "You can have a bite if you ask nicely."

She shook her head. "You can't tempt me. Lemon meringue's my favorite."

He stirred sugar and cream into his steaming mug. "So tell me your big news," he prompted.

For a moment, she thought he was referring to what had happened between her and Bryce. Her shock must have shown in her face.

"About the case?" Ricardo sounded puzzled. "Is there something else going on, as well?"

"N-no, of course not," Mari stuttered. She glanced around to make sure that no one could eavesdrop.

Four teenagers sat giggling in a booth across the room, a trucker hunched on a stool at the counter and a couple across the aisle appeared too engrossed in each other to notice anything less than an alarm going off.

Despite all that, Mari leaned forward and lowered her voice. "You have to keep this to yourself," she warned.

"Of course." With a solemn expression, Ricardo traced an X over his heart. "You have my word."

Briefly she explained about the prescriptions and the report that they'd been forged.

"So they don't suspect you anymore?" he asked. "That must be a wonderful feeling of relief."

Mari fiddled with her coffee mug. "I'll be relieved when the real thief is caught."

"Well, of course." He flashed her a brief smile. "Have you and your detective discussed who might be trying to frame you?"

His question made her mouth drop open. "Why would you ask that?"

"Think about it," he replied, cutting a bite of pie with his fork. "What better way for the guilty party to divert suspicion from himself than to direct it toward someone else."

She toyed with the meringue on her plate. "I'm sure there are people in town who don't like me for any number of reasons, as well as people who oppose the research center. They think fertility and stem-cell research are too controversial. That person would still need to have access to the supply cabinet, too."

He shrugged as he kept eating. "At least the heat should be off you, huh?"

Mari thought of the *heat* she and Bryce had generated the other night. "Let's hope so."

She changed the subject and they managed to keep the conversation light while they finished their pie. After Ricardo paid the check, he outlined a couple of his ideas for the center while they drove back to town. Mari was grateful for the diversion.

"I'll contact a friend in Baltimore," he promised as he pulled up next to her car, parked alone in the deserted lot. "He knows people who might have money to invest."

"Thanks. It was good to see you," Mari said as she dug out her keys.

He waited for her to unlock her door. "What's that on your windshield?" he asked. "It looks like a note."

Coming so closely after his comment about her being framed, the sight of the folded paper tucked under the wiper blade gave her a sudden chill. Frowning, she glanced quickly at the scrawled words. *Call my cell when you get this, B,* followed by a phone number.

Her relief was mixed with trepidation. "It's okay," she said. "Detective Collins wants me to contact him."

"What for?"

As much as she trusted Ricardo, she wasn't about to elaborate.

"Who knows? I'll call him on my way home." She gave Ricardo a platonic hug.

"You take care," he said, shutting her door for her. When she held up her cell phone, he waved and went back to his own car.

Mari waited until he had driven away before she punched in Bryce's number.

He answered on the first ring. "Where were you?"

"Don't I even get a hello before you start grilling me, Detective?" she asked.

"I'm not on duty, so you don't have to be formal." His deep voice sent a shiver of longing dancing across her nerve endings. Before she could think of a clever response, car lights switched on across the parking lot. They were aimed straight at Mari, spooking her.

"Um, where are you right now?" she whispered into the phone, as though someone could overhear.

"Why?" His tone was suddenly wary.

"It's probably nothing." Feeling silly, she tried to disguise her nervousness. "I'm sitting in the parking lot at work and someone just turned on their head-lights."

"That would be me," he replied. "I've been here waiting for you to get back."

Chapter Six

What a chump, Bryce told himself as he drove over to where Mari's car was parked. He hadn't meant to admit he'd been hanging around like a lovesick puppy, but when he saw her give that Phillipe character a hug, he'd experienced a surge of possessiveness.

What right did Bryce have to feel possessive of Mari? He had slept with her, not staked a claim.

He was unable to block the corrosive thoughts. Had she really come to the hospital to check on a patient, or to see the other man? But if they were involved, wouldn't she have kissed him goodbye? Maybe they were just friends, as she had insisted when Bryce had brought up the other doctor's name.

Bryce wasn't actually *jealous*. He just didn't care for her taste in men. Other men, at least.

By the time he pulled the Jag up next to her car, she was leaning against the fender with her hands braced on her trim hips.

"What's this, your date car?" she asked with a curl to her lip.

"Don't I get a hello before you grill me?" he quipped.

To his relief, her expression relaxed into a small grin. The beauty of it reached right down his throat and stole his breath from his lungs.

"Okay, a point for you." Wetting her fingertip, she traced an imaginary mark in the air. It was a game they'd played when they dated in school, giving each other points for winning a verbal exchange.

Unfortunately for Bryce, the sight of her tongue slipping out to touch her finger had never affected him this strongly before, not even when he'd been a testosterone-charged adolescent. His instinct warned him not to make a big deal out of the fact that she remembered.

"You didn't expect me to pick up chicks in the department sedan, did you?" he teased as she looked over the low-slung Jag. "Want a ride?"

She shook her head, although she did so with obvious reluctance. "I'd better not."

"How about tomorrow?" he asked, getting out of his car.

His blood was still humming. He would have liked to sweep her into his arms and make her forget about Dr. Phillipe, but if he did, she'd know immediately about his strong attraction to her.

But where had she gone with Dr. Phillipe, and for what reason? Could it be possible that the two of them were working together to steal Orcadol?

Bryce wouldn't be the first cop to be blinded from the truth by personal feelings. However, from what he'd seen of Mari over the last few weeks, he would bet his badge that she was no more capable of breaking the law than his mother.

"What do you mean, tomorrow?" she asked. "Have you got some news?"

"No. None of the information from your employee records has turned up anything yet. We're still looking." He rested his hands on her shoulders, feeling her tension. It matched his own and he could only hope she was equally frustrated by their earlier interruption.

"How's your patient doing?" he asked, trying not to sound suspicious.

Had there actually been a patient, or had it been the other man calling her?

"False alarm," she replied. "We sent her home."

If she wasn't telling the truth, she was a good actor. "Where did you and the doc go?" Bryce asked before he could prevent himself. Real subtle.

"A new café called The Buttercup. Have you been there?"

"I don't think so." The name didn't sound familiar. "Where's it located?"

"Out by the middle school."

He shook his head. "Guess not."

"They've got great pie," she said, "including strawberry-rhubarb."

It was his favorite. She'd baked him one when she was taking home ec, but the crust got burned. She was so upset that he'd had to eat the entire thing in order to make her feel better.

He couldn't resist a grin. "Nice of you to remember."

To his delight, her expression softened. "It was actually the sight of you choking down that whole pie that I couldn't forget," she teased.

He didn't know what to say, but then her smile wobbled. "That was so was sweet of you," she added softly.

It wasn't the moment to admit that he'd had to pull over to the side of the road and puke on his way home.

"Let's play hooky," he suggested instead, leaning down to look into her eyes. "We've both been working way too hard. I can use a break and I bet you can, too."

She searched his face. "What do you have in mind?"

At least she hadn't refused immediately. "We can

drive over to the next county,'' he suggested. ''There's bound to be something going on. Every little town has a weekend festival, a craft show or a farmer's market of some sort. What do you say?''

If he didn't touch her soon, he'd implode. Clenching his teeth, he settled for running his fingertips along the silky skin of her jaw. When she swallowed, the movement of her throat made him want to nibble a path down past the collar of her shirt.

Just thinking about it made his hand tremble, but she didn't seem to notice.

''A day trip would be fun.'' Longing ached in her voice. ''What would people think if they saw us together, though?''

''We're not exactly movie stars,'' he teased, as some of his tension drained away. ''Wear shades and a hat. We'll blend right in with the rest of the tourists.''

A sudden thought chilled him. ''Or did you already have plans?'' he asked.

''That's right, I've got a full weekend,'' she replied, snapping her fingers. ''I almost forgot.''

Disappointment sent his stomach plunging like a broken freight elevator. Why had he thought that an attractive, intelligent professional woman like Mari would be free at the last minute, just because she had slept with him on one occasion? ''Mind my asking what?''

''Laundry and vacuuming,'' she replied on a bubble of laughter that first relieved and then utterly charmed him. "I think they can wait."

On impulse, he grabbed her hand and lifted it to his lips. He nibbled on her fingers, making her giggle again before she pulled her hand free. "I'll pick you up at ten. How does that sound?"

"Are we taking your Jag, hotshot?"

"Why not? It's my date car, and we're going on a date, aren't we?" he asked.

"Sounds like one to me," she replied. "What are we getting ourselves into?"

Damned if he knew. "Just playing hooky," he said with a wink.

She appeared to be relieved. "I'd better go."

Bryce thought about kissing her, but he didn't want to do anything to make her change her mind about tomorrow. Reluctantly he balled his fists inside the pockets of his slacks.

"I'll see you in the morning," he said as she got behind the wheel.

"Good night."

He shut her door and she waggled her fingers at him before she drove away.

Even though he'd put in a lot of hours at work this week, Bryce doubted that he'd get much sleep as he waited for morning to arrive.

"I wonder if anyone recognized you," Mari said. The silver Jag had attracted the attention of a pair of bicyclists who stared with open admiration.

Just like in any small town, the residents of Binghamton loved to gossip, especially about Mari's prominent family. As she had recently found out, there was a fine line between news and notoriety.

She had been ready and waiting when he knocked on her door. As luck would have it, when they left together, one of her neighbors was outside watering her flowerpots and another was returning from walking his dog. Mari had waved to both without stopping to chat or to introduce Bryce. It would have been awkward if one of them had asked what he did for a living.

"I'm not Brad Pitt," he replied now as he pulled onto the main street. "Relax. No one recognized me."

She studied his profile. He was wearing fancy sunglasses and a grin that was downright devilish. A white T-shirt contrasted with his tanned arms. Gray shorts showed off his muscular thighs. His presence in the leather bucket seat next to hers was definitely affecting her breathing.

"Is that my cue to say that you're way cuter than Brad?" she cooed.

When he glanced at her, his smile deepened. "Only if you want me to point out that you're a lot sharper than you look."

Laughing, she slapped his tanned arm lightly. It was as though they'd agreed to put their concerns aside for the day. Getting away was a good idea. She needed some fun, and she couldn't think of a soul she'd rather be with.

"Thank you," she said sincerely.

"For what? All I've done so far is pick you up."

"You suggested this outing," she explained. "It's been a while since I've done something fun."

For a moment he rested his hand on her bare leg above her knee, causing a shiver of reaction. "I've got to stop for gas," he said, glancing at the gauges. "There's a place on the other side of town that's never very busy."

The corner of his mouth twitched. "We should be able to sneak in and back out again before anyone alerts the *National Tattler.*"

Without bothering to reply, Mari settled back against the seat. She had given herself permission to enjoy the day without wallowing in either guilt or doubt, or trying to figure out where their relationship was headed. To that end, she looked at the scenery with a feeling of contentment she hadn't experienced in a long time.

After a few minutes, he drove up to a gas pump in front of a run-down mini-mart. "Can I get you anything?" he asked as he got out of the Jag. "Some water? Coffee?"

"No, thanks." She rolled down her window while he pumped fuel into the tank.

The only other vehicle at the pumps was a rusty pickup truck towing an aluminum fishing boat. While she admired the way Bryce's snug T-shirt showed off the muscles of his chest and shoulders, a small car came in fast and squealed to a stop in front of the store. The little coupe was dirty, the back fender didn't match the rest of the paint and the muffler rattled.

Two men got out, both of them dressed in worn clothing. One tossed down a cigarette before heading into the store, but the other looked over at the Jag.

At the same time, Bryce bent down and poked his head through his open window. "So much for sneaking away unseen," he said quietly. "That's my brother who just pulled in."

She had known Joey slightly as a young kid. She hadn't been around him a lot, but she remembered that Bryce had always felt responsible for him.

She and Bryce hadn't gotten around to discussing their families, partly because the two clans had nothing in common. Bryce's father had worked in her family's coal mine until an accident disabled him.

"Hey, Bryce, my man!" came a loud shout.

"Great," she heard him mutter before he straightened.

As Joey jogged toward them across the parking lot, Mari suspected from his unsteadiness that, despite the early hour, he was either high or he'd been drinking.

"How ya doing, bro?" Joey demanded when he got to the driver's side of the car.

"Yeah, hi, Joey," Bryce said. He sounded resigned, his earlier good mood nowhere in evidence.

"When are you going to let me drive this bomb?" Joey whined. "You keep promising."

Bryce's bark of laughter lacked humor. "Wrong, *bro.* I'm not that crazy."

Joey thumped the fender so hard that Mari jumped, and then he bent down to look at her through the window.

Mari was shocked at how much he had changed, and not for the better. Did Bryce realize that his little brother had a drug problem? Of course he would. In his job he'd had plenty of experience identifying addicts.

"Hey, looks like you got a date," Joey exclaimed loudly, peering at Mari. As soon as he recognized her, his expression froze and he straightened up abruptly.

"What's she doing with you?" he demanded.

"Free country," Bryce replied as he replaced the gas nozzle. "Come on, Joey. We'll talk later, okay? I'll call you."

He was trying to back his brother away from the car.

Joey ducked around him and came around to the passenger side. He jabbed a finger at Mari's face.

"Don't think I forgot what your greedy, no-good family did to us," he shouted, his eyes blazing hatred.

Stunned, she pressed herself against the back of her seat.

"I'm sorry about your father," she replied, keeping her voice even, "but the accident wasn't our fault. The company did everything it could to help all of you." Perhaps that hadn't been entirely true, but she wasn't going to debate it with him now.

She'd only been a child herself when the mine accident happened. If Bryce also held the Binghams responsible, he'd never said so.

Joey's features twisted, and his next comment scorched her ears. Before he could add anything more, Bryce's hand clamped down on his shoulder and hauled him back from the window.

"That's enough!" His voice crackled with authority. "If your apology meant anything to Mari, I'd make you give her one. Lucky for you, she probably doesn't want to hear it."

Joey continued to glare at Mari until Bryce shifted to block him from her view. "You run along, and I'll talk to you later," Bryce told him. "Got it?"

Without bothering to reply, Joey turned his back and stomped over to his car.

Bryce leaned down to Mari. "You okay?"

She nodded as Joey got into the passenger side of the other car and slammed the door. "I'm sorry," she told Bryce.

"What for? You didn't do anything. It's no secret that he's always blamed your family for what happened to Dad. I don't want it to spoil our day, okay?"

There didn't seem to be anything more she could say without adding to his obvious embarrassment.

"Okay," she agreed, dragging up a smile that he appeared to accept at face value.

The car with Joey and his friend left the lot with a

squeal of tires that Bryce ignored. After he'd paid for the gasoline, he turned the Jag back onto the highway. For a few minutes, neither of them spoke.

"I've tried to help him," Bryce said abruptly. "I've gotten him jobs, which he promptly loses, I give him money. I think you and I both have a good idea what he spends it on." He sighed deeply, his gaze straight ahead.

"Joey lived with me for a while, but that didn't work out. I rented him a little house on the edge of town. He and his friends partied 24/7 until the land-lord finally evicted him. They trashed the place before they left, so a couple of the guys from work helped me with it."

"Where does he live now?" Mari asked, her heart going out to him at the sound of disappointment in his voice. He'd blame himself for failing Joey, she was sure.

He shrugged, his hands gripping the steering wheel so tightly that his knuckles were pale.

"Who knows? He moves constantly. I think he flops at someone's place until they get fed up and kick him out."

"He's not working?" she asked.

"His last regular job was at a car wash. The owner told me Joey was late a lot. Then he showed up high on something, so there was no choice but to let him go."

Bryce had probably gotten him the job in the first place, but Mari didn't want to ask.

Play the Lucky Hearts Game

and get...

2 FREE BOOKS
and a FREE MYSTERY GIFT...

yes! YOURS to KEEP!

I have scratched off the silver card. Please send me my *2 FREE BOOKS* and *FREE mystery GIFT*. I understand that I am under no obligation to purchase any books as explained on the back of this card.

Scratch Here!

then look below to see what your cards get you... 2 Free Books & a Free Mystery Gift!

335 SDL DZ5T

235 SDL DZ59

FIRST NAME

LAST NAME

ADDRESS

APT.#

CITY

STATE/PROV.

ZIP/POSTAL CODE

(S-SE-05/04)

Twenty-one gets you
2 FREE BOOKS
and a *FREE MYSTERY GIFT!*

Twenty gets you
2 FREE BOOKS!

Nineteen gets you
1 FREE BOOK!

TRY AGAIN!

BUSINESS REPLY MAIL
FIRST-CLASS MAIL   PERMIT NO. 717-003   BUFFALO, NY

POSTAGE WILL BE PAID BY ADDRESSEE

SILHOUETTE READER SERVICE
3010 WALDEN AVE
PO BOX 1867
BUFFALO NY 14240-9952

NO POSTAGE
NECESSARY
IF MAILED
IN THE
UNITED STATES

"I'm sorry." She didn't know what else to say.

"Me, too." He thumped the wheel lightly with the flat of his hand. "Until Joey stops blaming everyone else for his problems, there's not much I can do."

"But you'll keep trying to help him," Mari guessed.

"He's my brother." Clearly, that was all the reason Bryce needed.

Once again, the two of them fell silent. The road began to curve as they headed out of the valley. Mari tried to think of something else to say as they followed the incline into the hills, but she didn't want to mention the investigation.

"Where are we going?" she asked as they crossed the county line.

"The little towns up ahead always have a bunch of harvest festivals and things like that during this time of year," Bryce replied. "Haven't you ever been?"

Mari shook her head. "I haven't come out this way in a long while, but I think it's a great idea."

He appeared pleased by her comment. "I figured we'd look around, grab some lunch and check out what else there is going on. Does that work for you?"

She wanted to tell him that as long as he was with her, it worked just fine. "Maybe I'll see a birthday present for Grandma. I haven't gotten her anything yet."

He didn't reply. There had been tension between him and her family when she was dating him before, especially when her parents found out that he opposed her going to college. She knew that her father had been relieved when she and Bryce broke up.

She wanted to ask about Bryce's parents, but she held back. His father's mine injury had always been a touchy subject. She was loyal to her father, but privately she hated her family's involvement in the coal industry. Geoff had worked hard to diversify their holdings. For that, Mari was especially grateful.

"What are you thinking about?" Bryce asked. "You're so quiet."

He slowed down as they passed through a small town. It consisted of nothing more than a gas station, a few houses, a grocery store and a bar.

A hand-lettered sign on the shoulder of the road said Squash And Punkins. Fresh Zuckinis. A woman sat at a small table beneath an umbrella. Next to her were baskets and mounds of yellow, orange and green blobs. At her feet, a large hound dozed in the sun.

"I was thinking about your family," Mari admitted.

When Bryce sped up again, she wasn't sure whether it was because they had left the tiny burg behind them or if her comment upset him.

"They're fine," he said before she could ask any questions, his tone indicating clearly that the subject was closed.

"I'm glad to hear that." Part of Mari wanted to talk about the past, to find out how their breakup had affected him. There was so much she still didn't understand, but she told herself that what happened was so long ago that it no longer mattered.

"Do you ever see Kurt or Billie?" she asked instead. They had played football with Bryce. "I've lost touch with so many of the kids, especially those who moved away."

For a little while they talked about their classmates, bringing each other up to date. Mari was shocked to hear that one was dead and two were serving time. Bryce hadn't known that the class clown was married with seven children, including two sets of twins.

The next town they arrived at was larger. A big hand-painted sign, decorated with balloons and streamers, advertised the harvest festival, craft fair and visiting carnival.

"This is more like it," Bryce said enthusiastically. "Shall we check it out?"

"Works for me." Mari could see a Ferris wheel and the tops of tents above a row of trees in a nearby field. A larger produce stand had been set up at one end of the main street. Next to it was a vendor selling baskets.

A sign with an arrow directed them to keep going through the downtown area, which was three blocks long. The sidewalks were full of people wearing shorts, sun hats and sandals, looking in shop windows.

Mari could see more balloons and people up ahead. A man in a bright orange vest stood in the middle of the street, directing traffic. Bryce found an empty spot and they left the car.

Immediately the sound of music from the carnival and the aroma of frying food assailed Mari's senses. People were everywhere.

"Which way first?" Bryce asked, grabbing her hand. "Are you hungry?"

She wanted to stand still for a moment and savor the feeling of being connected to him again. Instead she smiled.

"Cotton candy?" she asked.

His eyes seemed to darken. "Blue?" he guessed correctly.

She'd had a thing about blue cotton candy, insisting that it tasted different from pink. Now she was pleased that he remembered, but she tried to ignore just how many memories they shared, some little and sweet, others important and hurtful.

Someone bumped against her and she realized she was blocking the pathway.

"Yes, blue," she replied with a laugh. "Absolutely."

Glancing around, he tugged on her hand. "Let's go this way."

Together they headed for the row of trailers where the food vendors were set up amidst the sounds of noisy generators and shouted voices hawking a variety of treats.

"Be careful," Bryce said as he guided her over power cables and around trash barrels.

They passed stalls selling bowls of savory burgoo, a thick stew made with a variety of different meats cooked with okra, potatoes and spices. There was also corn on the cob, snow cones, funnel cakes, ice cream on a stick and corn dogs. Smoke rose from a barbecue grill in the far corner.

In front of the stalls were rows of picnic tables, half of their benches full of people. A clown wandered through the crowd hawking a shining bunch of Mylar balloons. A baby cried. Children laughed and a fiddler played.

Finally they found what they were looking for, a cart with a huge pot of lemonade, bright yellow orbs bobbing in the liquid. Next to it was a row of cotton candy.

Bryce bought the last blue one. When he presented the paper cone to Mari with a gallant bow, she felt an unexpected rush of emotion.

"Thanks." She was glad her sunglasses hid the sudden moisture that blurred her vision. "Aren't you having any?"

"I'll settle for the lemonade. Would you like some?"

Flustered by her feelings, all Mari could do was to shake her head before taking a mouthful of fluffy spun sugar from the paper cone she was holding. By the time Bryce had gotten his drink and a straw, she'd regained her composure.

"Now where to?" he asked. "The Ferris wheel?"

"You know better than that," she replied without

thinking. The combination of height and circling always made her ill, but she hadn't meant to indicate that she expected him to remember every little thing about her.

"Sissy," he said lightly, recapturing her free hand. "I saw some craft booths over there." He motioned with his head.

"Terrific." Mari took another bite of cotton candy, doing her best to ignore the way he wrapped his lips around the straw to his drink. "Grandma loves honeysuckle, so maybe I can find her some fancy soaps." She thought of Milla. "And a baby gift for one of the midwives who's expecting."

As she browsed, Bryce was surprisingly patient. He trailed after her through the stalls selling jewelry, quilts and homemade jam. While she was looking at little clay pots, he stopped to examine some hand-painted saw blades. When she glanced up, he was talking to the artist. The old man had long hair, a flowing white beard and a corncob pipe clamped in his teeth.

After a few moments, Mari wandered across the aisle to a table full of cookies and fudge.

"Would you like a sample?" one of the teenagers asked, holding out a plate. "We're raising money for our soccer team."

"Thanks." The square of fudge melted on her tongue, so she bought a box to take back to the clinic.

Bryce was still talking to the saw-blade artist, but there was a booth selling soap right next door. She found just what she wanted, bars of honeysuckle arranged in a little basket. It was wrapped in pretty gold-tinted cellophane that was tied with a bow.

"Mari!" Bryce's hand came down on her shoulder, startling her. "For a moment I didn't know where you'd gone."

When she looked into his face, he appeared almost angry. She couldn't see his eyes behind his tinted lenses, but his cheeks were flushed and his mouth was set in a grim line.

"I'm sorry," she said, embarrassed. "I thought you saw me come over here."

His harsh expression relaxed, and he released his grip on her shoulder.

"No, I'm sorry," he replied. "I was just worried when I looked up and you weren't there."

A memory flashed through her mind of a country fair when they'd been separated and he had searched for twenty minutes before he'd found her. Was he thinking of that, too, or was most of the time they'd spent together a half-forgotten blur?

"Forgive me?" he asked lightly.

"I never hold a grudge against a man who buys me cotton candy," she replied.

To her surprise, he leaned down and kissed her lips. "Any time."

She might have dismissed the gesture, but his deep, thick tone made her wish she knew better how he felt. Tossing his empty cup into a trash barrel, he laced his fingers through hers. The crowd had increased, as had the temperature. An older woman jostled him as she walked by with a friend, too busy chatting to notice.

"Have you seen everything you wanted to?" he asked Mari. "If you still like catfish, there's a restaurant I know of right on the river where we could go for a late lunch."

She hadn't realized how hungry she was. "That sounds heavenly."

After she had stopped to throw away her cone and rinse her sticky hands under a faucet, they worked their way back to his car. She hadn't seen a soul she recognized, but several women noticed Bryce. They gave him long looks he either didn't see or chose to ignore. One of them, an attractive redhead, caught Mari's eye and winked.

"You didn't even realize what a stir you caused, did you?" she asked him after they got back into the Jag.

"Huh?" He gave her a confused look as he backed out of the parking spot. "What do you mean?"

Not wanting to distract him and cause an accident, she waited until they had driven through the knots of pedestrians crossing the street in every direction.

"The women were staring," Mari teased, curious to see his reaction. "You're quite a hunk, Detective, even without the badge."

To her disappointment, he didn't reply, even though she could see a blush spread along his cheekbones. She waited silently, but he didn't say anything at all until they'd left the fair behind them. Then, to her surprise, he pulled off the road into an overgrown driveway.

"Where are we going?" she asked as they bounced to a stop.

Bryce set the brake and then he put his sunglasses on the dashboard. With an unreadable expression, he removed hers, as well. Suddenly the tension in the car was as thick as maple syrup.

"Do *you* think I'm a hunk, Marigold?" he asked.

She couldn't have been more surprised if he'd started singing their high-school fight song.

"W-what?" she stuttered.

He curved his hand along her jaw, his gaze narrowed and intent.

"Are you attracted to me?" he repeated.

She spoke without thinking. "I slept with you, didn't I?"

He continued to study her face as though he was memorizing it.

"But I still haven't figured out why," he mumbled.

As soon as his meaning sank in, her temper flared like a rocket. She jerked away, so offended that she was shaking all over.

"If you weren't a cop, I'd slap your face for suggesting that I did it to stay out of jail!" she cried.

He went blank with obvious astonishment.

"Oh, God, no!" he exclaimed, reaching for her. "That's not what I meant at all."

Near tears, Mari pressed against the passenger door

and batted his hands away. Granted, she hadn't been proud of her actions, but neither had she had any ulterior motives.

"Leave me alone."

A muscle jumped in his cheek. "Not for a minute."

He rested one hand gently on her knee, and she had no room to pull away. "Now listen to me, okay?" He waited while she glared at him.

"Start talking," she said coldly, eyeing his hand with as much distaste as she could possibly show. Part of her wanted to wail that their lovely day was being spoiled.

He appeared to weigh his words carefully before he started speaking.

"You would never sleep with me when we were going together," he said carefully. "I was a little surprised, that's all."

His hand tightened on her leg and his voice dropped a notch. "I never for one moment figured you for the kind of woman who would attempt to manipulate me. Get that idea out of your head right now, *Doctor*."

His tone had taken on an edge, as though he was the one who was insulted.

Mari paid little heed to the tears that spilled from her eyes and ran down her cheeks. She'd really made a hash of things.

"Why are you crying?" he asked with a frown. At least his voice had lost its angry edge.

She pressed her lips tightly together to stop their trembling.

"Just because I was embarrassed at the idea you might think I was easy at best and scheming at worst, I insulted you." She held back a sob. "I'm sorry."

He leaned closer. "Answer me one thing," he said solemnly.

"What's that?" He probably wanted to know if she had bus money because he intended leaving her here, she thought.

The corners of his mouth lifted. "Do you think I'm a hunk?"

Chapter Seven

The intensity of Bryce's expression made Mari catch her breath.

"That's my secret," she replied.

His gaze shifted to her mouth and she thought he was going to kiss her. She leaned forward, her heart racing with expectation, but Bryce straightened abruptly.

"I guess we'd better go get something to eat," he said in a husky voice.

Before Mari could collect her scattered wits, he released the brake and began to back the car around. Why had he wanted her to admit that she still found him to be the most attractive man with whom she had ever been involved?

Could he not tell how she felt from the way she reacted to him? She had been afraid that her desire had been as transparent as glass, but perhaps it wasn't so obvious to him.

With her hands clasped tightly in her lap, she mulled over the idea that he might not be as cocky as he appeared. Could it be possible that beneath the confident mask, he was as afraid of being hurt again as she?

"Why so quiet?" he asked after a few moments, his attention focused on the curving road ahead of them. It followed the river that meandered like a flat blue ribbon beyond a ragged screen of trees.

Mari wasn't ready to ask what he wanted from her. She hadn't yet sorted out her own feelings.

"I guess my mind was wandering," she replied with a smile. "It's that kind of day."

If he was disappointed by her answer, he didn't let it show.

"I hope you're hungry," he said instead as he flipped on his turn signal and downshifted.

Next to the driveway where he turned in was a sign advertising a boat launch, picnic area and cabins for rent. Just beyond it was a long, low building with smoke pouring from its chimney.

Catfish Jack's said the sign on the roof. The parking lot was full of cars and most of the outdoor tables were occupied.

"They look busy," Mari said as he pulled into an empty slot.

"I called ahead," he replied before getting out of the car.

Mari waited while he came around to her side and opened her door. Back in school, the other boys' teasing about his manners hadn't seemed to bother him. *Blame my mother,* he'd always replied with a grin.

"It doesn't look like the type of place to take reservations," Mari observed as she stood by his side.

The people she could see were dressed as casually as she and Bryce in their shorts and sandals. The building wasn't exactly falling down, but its dark green exterior could have used a fresh coat of paint.

"I called from my cell while you were picking out soap." Bryce led her up the wood steps. "Jack and I go way back."

There wasn't time to ask questions before the hostess, a pretty teenager wearing braces and a long dress, greeted them with a smile. She led them through the restaurant to a table on a screened porch overlooking the river. The sound of the water was like background music.

"Is this okay?" she asked Bryce.

"Perfect. Thanks, Teresa." He winked as he pulled out Mari's chair.

"Daddy's not here," the hostess said as she handed them menus. "He's at a stock sale over in Danville, but I'll be sure to tell him you came by."

"I've never heard of this place," Mari whispered after Teresa left with their drink order. "How long has it been open?"

"It's a fixture," he replied, tapping his finger on the plastic tablecloth with its checkered red-and-white pattern. "Not what you're used to?"

The disparity between his blue-collar background and her family's success had always rubbed at him, no matter how many times she insisted that it wasn't important.

"Still think I'm a snob?" she asked lightly as she unfolded her paper napkin. "I'll have you know that I've eaten a burger at South Junction now and then."

"I never thought you were a snob, but this is a step up from a burger joint," he said dryly.

An embarrassed flush warmed her cheeks, but she didn't want to start an argument. "You know I didn't mean it that way."

He started to say something, but their waitress appeared with two sweating glasses of iced tea. She was an older woman with startling dyed black hair and she wore a checkered uniform that matched the tablecloth.

"Hi, Bryce," she said warmly. "You want the usual?"

He glanced at Mari. "Did you want some more time to look at the menu?"

"You're the expert," she said sweetly, still smarting from his comment. "Why don't you order for me?"

He handed the menus to the waitress. "Two specials, Helen, with extra tartar."

"Coming right up."

"Sound good?"

She arched her eyebrow. "You know I have no idea what you just ordered."

"Fried catfish, hush puppies, slaw and homemade tartar sauce," he recited.

She folded her hands in her lap, smoothing out the napkin. "That will be just fine."

During the meal, which was every bit as good as he'd promised, they kept the conversation light, like people on a first date. Mari was surprised to find out that they still had so much in common.

They shared a fondness for watching tennis on television and mindless action movies with dazzling special effects. Both preferred reading to video games. They disagreed on politics, but were interested in local county government.

Over dessert, a mouthwatering blueberry cobbler that they shared, they argued about economic growth and preserving the environment. Mari tended to agree with most of Bryce's opinions, but she wasn't going to give in easily. She was having too much fun making him work to defend his position.

When Helen brought the check and Bryce dug out his wallet, Mari was surprised to realize how much she had enjoyed herself.

"This has been fun," she told him as they left the restaurant hand in hand. "Thank you."

"The day's not over," he said when they got to the car. "Do you have to get back to Binghamton at any special time?"

The hours with Bryce had flown and Mari was surprised to see that it was already late afternoon. Except for feeding Lennox and doing her laundry, she was free until the next morning, but she wasn't about to admit it.

"What did you have in mind?" she asked instead.

His grip tightened on her hand, and he looked over at the sign by the road with a meaningful expression.

Boat launch, picnic area, cabins for rent. She knew what he was suggesting. His intention was in his eyes.

She swallowed hard. What had happened between them in her office had been spontaneous, an unplanned flare of desire that neither of them had been able to ignore. Going with him now would be different.

A deliberate choice.

She didn't know what to say. After a moment, a muscle twitched in his cheek and he looked away.

"Come on," he said, voice thick. "I'll take you home."

Mari was tempted to grab the easy way out.

Instead, she asked, "Is there a path along the river? Could we take a walk?"

He turned back to her with his car keys gripped tightly in one hand. His face was unreadable, his gaze piercing.

"Is that what you want?"

"It's been a wonderful day," she replied softly,

touching his forearm. His skin was warm beneath her fingers. A feeling of yearning, more complex than the simple flush of desire she had felt before, rose up inside her. "I'm not ready for it to end."

His hard expression relaxed into a smile that lit his eyes. "Me, neither." He pocketed his keys and they walked past the restaurant toward the water.

The path, wide enough for two, led them to the riverbank. It was an easy walk and Mari recognized many of the native shrubs and flowers. Ferns were mixed with wild iris, buttercups and daisies. A breeze blew off the water and trees shaded sections of the path.

As pleasant as it was to walk with Bryce and let the peaceful atmosphere wash over her, Mari knew they needed to talk. Eventually they came to a fork in the path with a narrow offshoot that wandered through a thick stand of trees.

"Could we go down there?" she asked.

Bryce gave her a searching look before he nodded. They had to walk single file, so she went on ahead. After a few minutes she found what she was looking for, an aged wood bench in a tiny clearing where they could have a private conversation.

"Let's sit here for a minute," she suggested.

When Bryce joined her on the bench, he left a foot of space between them and his expression was guarded. She reached for his hand. His firm grip gave her a boost of confidence.

"You were thinking about using one of the cabins, weren't you?" she asked softly.

Goodness, but she'd look like a fool if the thought had never occurred to him!

He appeared startled, making her stomach dip alarmingly with the fear that he might deny it. His hand tightened on hers, and he shifted so that he was facing her.

"It seemed like a great idea." His voice was husky, but his gaze was steady. "Not that it was something that I took for granted," he added hastily. "I don't want you to feel pressured."

She started to shake her head, but he lifted their joined hands and rubbed the back of hers against the side of his face.

"Ever since that night, I've missed you, Marigold. You're all I think about. I can't get you out of my head, no matter how hard I try."

His admission stunned her. That kind of openness deserved the same from her in return.

"I wanted to talk about that," she said haltingly. "To explain, or try to, that being swept away is different than looking you in the face today and agreeing to, um, to *this* when I'm not, when we aren't…"

She stumbled to a halt, her face flaming, with no idea how to finish what she had started.

"When you're not so caught up in the moment that you can't stop yourself?" he asked grimly.

"Yes. No." She waved her free hand. "I want you, too," she blurted. "It's just—"

Before she could finish, he leaned over and kissed her. Her mind blanked, and she slid her arms around his neck. Her breasts pressed against his chest and his body felt so good that she could hardly keep from arching closer still.

Before she'd had nearly enough of him, he broke the connection. To her surprise, he was grinning, even though his breathing was shallow.

"So you've got the hots for me, too," he said, "but calmly renting a room isn't your style?"

"I don't know about the 'calmly' part," she muttered, looking away.

"Oh, honey, you don't know how happy I am to hear that."

He wrapped his arm around her shoulders, cuddling her to his side. Automatically, she hugged his waist.

"All day I kept wanting to toss you over my shoulder and head for the nearest motel," he continued, "but I didn't want you to think that a romp between the sheets was all I wanted."

"Is it?" she asked solemnly. The second the words were out, she wanted to call them back.

He turned to face her. "Right now I have to say that it's a big part of it."

Mari felt as though he had plunged a knife into her. She couldn't breathe.

"Well, I guess that's honest," she gasped, near tears.

"Look," he said forcefully, "there's so much else going on between us and around us right now. Who knows what either of us wants to happen. I don't have a crystal ball on me, do you?"

Silently she shook her head.

He swallowed hard, the muscles working in his tanned throat.

"What we shared was like nothing I've ever felt with anyone," he said hoarsely. "You're incredible. I haven't been able to think about much else and it's making me crazy." He paused to drop a quick kiss on her mouth. "I'm not going to lie to you or give you a bunch of pretty words that might not mean anything later on. Is that enough for you? Because if it isn't, be straight with me."

"And what if it isn't enough?" Mari asked, thinking that working together to catch a thief was going to be damned awkward either way.

"Then I'll probably shoot myself," he said gruffly, his gaze shifting.

She followed the direction of his gaze to stare at a huge old dogwood tree while she thought about what he'd told her. Instead of making promises in an effort to get what he wanted, he appeared to be doing his best to level with her. What more could she ask?

"Bryce," she said softly, waiting until she had his attention again, "do you think it's too late to rent one of those cabins?"

If Mari had pulled a gun from her purse and aimed it at his head, Bryce couldn't have been more surprised than when she asked about the cabin. A moment before, he'd been figuring that any chance of making love with her in the foreseeable future had just floated away like a dead branch down the river.

Now he quickly decided that the two of them had done enough talking. He wasn't sure what he'd said to change her mind, but he sure as hell wasn't going to chance making some fool-assed comment that would switch it right back again.

Taking time only to kiss her thoroughly, he led her back up the path, trying his damnedest not to break into a run or mow down the tourists coming at them from the other direction. He hustled Mari into the car, praying silently for a vacancy as they drove down the road to the little row of cabins nestled along the riverbank.

The cabins were used mostly by fishermen. Bait and lures were sold at the office, but there were no amenities such as a play area, a pool or a café other than Jack's. It wasn't all that surprising that one of the cabins was empty.

"Have you stayed here before?" Mari asked after he paid and came back to the car with a key.

Did she wonder whether he had brought other women?

"I stayed here once by myself," he replied. "There was a fire at the restaurant, so I took a few days of vacation and came over to help."

"Was anyone hurt?" Mari appeared genuinely concerned.

He shook his head as he drove to the last cabin and

parked. The last thing he wanted to discuss right now was anything that didn't involve undressing.

"There was a grease fire right after closing, but everyone got out."

"How did you meet Jack in the first place?" she asked after he opened her door.

"I pulled him over for a DUI while I was still on patrol," he said, sensing her hesitation to go inside. "I was young and righteous, so I gave him a hell of a lecture about his family and his business. After he'd gotten some counseling, he looked me up so he could thank me. Even better, he offered me a free meal. I come back when I can."

To his surprise, she stepped closer, putting her palms against his chest. Immediately his heart began thudding. His blood left his head in a rush.

"You're a nice man under that hard-as-nails exterior."

"Hard as nails is right," he said dryly.

Mari threw back her head and laughed in obvious delight.

"Sounds serious," she purred in a throaty voice as she slanted him a sexy look through her lashes. "Don't worry, sir. I'm a doctor. Let's get you inside so I can examine you and make sure everything still works."

Bryce wasn't about to argue. He fumbled the key with fingers that shook, dropping it before he finally managed to get the door unlocked. He prayed the room wasn't a dump. He told himself that all he wanted was a bed, but part of him wished it was a palace, for her.

"At least it's clean," he said when he saw the room.

"It's fine." Her voice sounded breathy with nerves.

Before he could search her face for signs of second thoughts, she snaked her arms around his neck and tipped back her head. When her hips brushed his arousal, he nearly lost it.

He gritted his teeth, determined this time to show her more than an adolescent rush of desire. "Whoa," he said softly, holding her still with his hands on her hips. "Let's take it slow this time."

She didn't reply, but her eyes were big in her face. Her cheeks were pink, her lips slightly parted.

Bryce struggled to follow his own suggestion. The first kiss he gave her was hardly more than a nibble when what he wanted was to gulp her down in one bite. She responded with a dreamy sigh. Her fingers brushed the back of his neck as her breasts nudged his chest. Her hair smelled faintly of lemons and her skin tasted of sunshine.

Miraculously, the urge to take that pushed him like the blade of a bulldozer slackened off and became an urge to lead, to share, to give.

He led her to the bed. Standing beside it, he unbuttoned her shirt and kissed his way down her throat. When her tempting curves were laid bare above a wisp of lavender bra with a front clasp tucked between her breasts, he nearly abandoned the plan to go slowly. Clenching his jaw, he forced himself to undo the buttons all the way to the hem. When he finished, she shimmied her shoulders and let the shirt slide down her arms to the floor.

Before allowing himself to unhook her bra, he captured her fingers in his and bent to kiss her knuckles. She pressed her lips to his temple. Swallowing hard, he freed her breasts, cradling their weight in his hands.

"Pretty," he murmured hoarsely.

Gently he plucked at the rosy nipples, pleased by her moan. Supporting her with his arm, he bent her backward and feasted.

The motion pressed her lower body right against his as he squeezed his eyes shut and hissed in a breath. Mari yanked his shirt up. While he fumbled it over his head, she skated her fingers up his bare ribs.

Her touch sent his game plan up in smoke. They quickly shed the rest of their clothing, and he stripped off the bedspread.

He sat on the edge of the bed with a hazy idea of drawing her between his legs. Instead she pushed him onto his back and crawled on top of him.

"I'm trying to go slow," he gasped, "but you're making it damned hard."

"I think we covered that," she responded with a giggle. "The doc's going to check that out."

What she did next scrambled his senses, blurred his

vision and almost shattered his control. It took every scrap of grit he had to make sure she was ready.

"Please, please," she implored him, arching against his hand.

It was all he needed to hear before he claimed her.

"Now I know why they call it afternoon delight," Mari murmured brazenly as she ran her hand over Bryce's wide back.

The room was still warm and they hadn't yet bothered to dress. The light from outside was filtered by the dark plaid window curtains that matched the worn bedspread. The wall paneling, she noticed for the first time, was knotty pine.

Bryce lay on his stomach next to her, his muscles as lax as a big cat's. His skin felt hot and damp from their lovemaking and his hand splayed on her hip was pleasantly heavy.

"I may never move again," he said on a groan of contentment.

Mari was stretched out on her side, limp and satiated. He was a clever and creative lover, as well as a patient one. Just thinking about the shattering response he'd drawn from her was enough to fan the flames of fresh desire.

When her hand slid lower to stroke his compact butt, he opened one eye.

"Are you trying to start something?" His voice was husky as he rolled onto his side to face her.

"I thought you were worn out," she teased. When

she glanced down, fresh desire spiraled through her. "Guess I was wrong."

"You're going to be the death of me yet," he replied as he pulled her beneath him.

Trembling with anticipation, she parted her legs and lifted her hips to meet his first powerful stroke. As he drove into her with single-minded intensity, she gripped his shoulders.

This time he wasn't patient. His hard thrusts made the box springs squeak in protest.

The tide of her passion rose like a breaking wave that crested almost immediately. He kept on relentlessly until it built again and she arched against him. This time his body clenched, his face pressed against her neck to muffle his hoarse shout. Together they soared.

He was still inside her, her legs wrapped around his waist and his arms holding her close when he rolled to his side. Her thigh was cushioned by the well-used mattress. After a moment, as her heart and her body calmed, she raised her hand to stroke the damp hair off his forehead.

Gradually his eyelids drifted shut, his breathing slowed and his mouth went slack. His hand rested on her hip and the care fell away from his face. While his chest rose and fell, slow and steady, she watched the square of light in the window fade.

There was something to be said for sizzling, uncomplicated lust between consenting adults, she thought with a secretive smile, pleased that he hadn't yet gotten enough of her.

She ignored the pang of worry that he would.

She had blocked all thoughts of the investigation from her mind today, and she wasn't about to ruin her mood by analyzing her feelings or speculating about his.

After a little while, she pushed against his shoulder.

"Hey," she said softly as he groaned a protest. "Come on, big boy, wake up."

His eyes flew open, still clouded by dreams. Blinking, he flopped onto his back and scrubbed his hand over his jaw.

"I can't believe I fell asleep," he muttered. "You could have picked my pockets, and I wouldn't have had a clue."

"If you had pockets." She sat on the edge of the bed and sent him a coy glance over her bare shoulder, doing her best to ignore her reaction to the sight of him sprawled on the sheets. "Makes me wonder who you're used to sleeping with, Detective."

Without waiting for a reply, she grabbed her clothes and went into the tiny bathroom, closing the door firmly behind her.

There was a spider in the shower and the towel hanging next to it looked thin enough to see through. Washing quickly, she finger-combed her hair and came back out fully dressed.

Bryce was stepping into his sandals, and he was humming. If she'd expected him to hustle her from the cabin with casual efficiency, she was mistaken. Instead he circled the bed and took her into his arms.

"I've had a great time," he said, smiling down at her, "and not just in this room. The entire day has been more fun than I've had in a long while."

He seemed so sincere that she didn't know what to say. Her feelings were still in a jumble, so she opted for a teasing remark to keep things light.

"Trying to get me to drop my guard?" she quipped with a laugh as she pulled out of his embrace.

She could tell from his fleeting expression of disappointment that her comment had fallen flat. He almost looked hurt.

"I just wanted you to know what I thought, before we get back to business as usual." His tone had leveled out, revealing nothing, but a muscle jerked in his cheek.

While she was trying to figure out what to say, he tossed the key on the bed and opened the front door. "Ready?"

She knew from his unsmiling expression that her suspicion had been right. She'd managed to upset him.

Way to go, Bingham. Wordlessly she followed him to the car and got inside, feeling awful. The shared warmth from their day had turned into an awkward chill. It was the last thing she wanted.

Nibbling on her lip, she waited while he drove back past Catfish Jack's, waving to Teresa on the porch, and turned onto the main highway. As he pressed down on the gas pedal, he appeared to be deeply pre-occupied, as though he had forgotten all about Mari's presence.

When she reached over to cover his hand with hers, he seemed startled by the gesture. It was too late for her to simply say that she, too, had enjoyed herself. An apology would only make things more awkward. She couldn't very well explain that her lame attempt at humor had been her way of protecting herself from taking his comment too seriously. She needed to *show* him that she was sorry for dismissing his sincerity.

"My grandma's birthday party is tomorrow," she said. "There's going to be a catered picnic on the grounds of her house in the afternoon. Would you like to come with me?"

Chapter Eight

Bryce didn't know what to say in response to Mari's unexpected invitation. Didn't she realize how awkward it would be for him if word spread that they were seeing each other socially? The fact that they'd been sleeping together compromised his principles enough, even though no one else knew about it. He was reluctant to remind her that she was still a person of interest in the case.

"Uh, I don't know if that's a good idea," he said, stumbling. "Your family was never too thrilled that you were seeing me the first time around."

To Bryce, *not too thrilled* was a gross understatement, like calling The Kentucky Derby *a little horse race.* The fact that he had been a high-school jock with decent grades and a part-time job mattered less than a hill of beans to the snooty Bingham clan. Perversely, they seemed to blame him for breaking the heart of their little princess, even though Mari was the one who couldn't get away from Binghamton, and Bryce, quick enough.

What her family should have done was thank him for not standing in the way of her fancy career!

"Bryce," Mari said now, cutting across his wandering thoughts, "are you going to explain just why attending Grandma's party wouldn't be a good idea, or leave me to guess?" She sounded annoyed, like royalty surprised by a lowly peasant's failure to appreciate the honor bestowed on him.

Well, perhaps that wasn't quite fair.

"Does she know you're inviting me?" he hedged, slowing for an SUV making a left turn.

"No, but why should it matter? I don't clear my dates with her." Her lips were dangerously close to pouting. "I thought it might be fun for you to see everyone."

Did she think he'd been living in a cave all this time? He'd seen the members of her family through the years. Whenever his path had crossed with one of theirs, they usually gave him a startled glance or a subdued nod before looking quickly away.

"I ran into your brother a few years ago when his apartment was burglarized," Bryce drawled, unable to keep the sarcasm from his tone. "He didn't seem especially chatty. Oh, now I remember, I was the one too busy writing up the report to exchange stock tips with him.''

Geoff had been openly hostile, causing the deputy with Bryce to ask later about what had been Geoff's problem.

Annoyed by the insurance forms he'd have to complete, had been Bryce's reply.

"Why are you acting like this?" Mari demanded. "If you don't want to go, just say so!"

"I don't want to go, okay?"

She turned away, but not before he saw the moisture shining in her eyes. Silently he cursed himself as she dug sunglasses from her purse and donned them.

During high school, the differences in their backgrounds had never seemed to matter except when his after-school job kept them apart. For him, attending college wasn't an option, nor was tagging along after her to hold down a menial job while she attended class. He couldn't bear the idea of watching the love in her eyes grow dim as she compared him to the hotshot college boys competing for her attention.

He'd kept silent while she made plans, putting off—until the day she left—the news that he wasn't going with her. Naturally she had been angry and confused.

Had he given up too easily? Had their love been strong enough for them to find a way if they had tried?

How many times had he tormented himself by picturing a face-off between them, him in a dishwasher's uniform and her dressed for some fancy school event? While she tried to make clueless Bryce understand that it was over between them, her date lounged against his sports car with a smirk on his face.

"Well, I guess I know where I stand, don't I?" she asked now. Her voice had the faintest tremor.

Once again he'd blown it with his silence. His frustration spilled over.

"What does *that* mean?"

They crossed the county line and passed the minimart where they'd run into Joey that morning. He had been high again. Bryce would have to find the time to connect with his brother and demand to know what kind of trouble Joey had found this time.

Bryce hadn't been by the folks' house to change the oil in his mother's car as he'd promised her last week, or to mow the lawn. A headache nagged at his temples.

"I'm not good enough for you to be seen with unless I'm wearing handcuffs," Mari sniffed.

Bryce stared, trying to recall the last thing he'd said. "Where did you get that idea?"

"You're impossible," she huffed, folding her arms across her chest. "I can't talk to you. You don't listen! That's always been our problem."

The pain in his head tightened like a vise crushing his temples.

"My problem is trying to carry on a rational conversation with someone who's totally *irrational*," he growled, nearly forgetting to slow down when he entered the Binghamton city limits. It would be just his luck to add a speeding ticket to his list of irritants. "When it comes to being totally unreasonable, you haven't changed a bit!"

"Me?" Mari huffed. "You're trying to shift the blame, refusing to take responsibility—just like you always did!" She folded her arms. "Well, this time it won't wash, buster."

"You're talking in riddles." He stopped at the four-way, waiting impatiently for an elderly driver to figure out that it was her turn. "You can't always have everything your way, just because your family owns the entire town."

"Now you're the one who's not making sense." Her face was in profile, her chin thrust out. "I'll have you know that I've worked hard for everything I've ever gotten. Medical school was no walk in the park and neither is directing the clinic."

Suddenly he realized that he had no idea what they were arguing about. They'd strayed so far from the original subject that he'd forgotten what it was. All he knew was that he was losing Mari again.

He turned onto her street, approaching her building from the back, and pulled into an empty spot. Before she could attempt to open her door and leap out of the car as he suspected that she might, he hit the automatic lock.

When her head whipped around, her eyes were

nearly shooting sparks. "Let me out or I'll start screaming."

"We'll both look like idiots," he warned. Nothing like the promise of keeping a low profile to tame a situation.

"I don't care! Unlock this door right now." She gave it a whack with her fist.

He suspected that she'd rather be hitting him.

"I'm sorry," he said, deliberately lowering his voice as he ignored the pounding in his head. "Let's not ruin a terrific day, okay? I'm sorry."

She glared at him for another moment. "Sorry for what?" she asked petulantly.

He knew from watching Oprah when he was home with the flu last winter that he'd be a fool to address that question. No second guesses allowed. Diversion was his best bet.

He extended his hand, palm up. "Truce?" He tried to appear remorseful, even though he had no idea what he'd done to make her mad. As far as he was concerned, they were equally guilty for running things into the ditch.

She looked at his hand as though it were a venomous snake. The lone tear track on her cheek tore at his heart.

"I don't know where we're headed," she said in a solemn little voice. "It's scary as hell."

The admission rattled him. Since that first time they had come together like a head-on collision, he had been entirely too busy scheming to get her back into the sack and the sooner, the better, to think past the end of his...nose.

A voice in his head told him admitting to that wouldn't be wise.

"I'm afraid, too." At least that was the truth. The possibility that she'd refuse to see him again scared the bejesus out of him. "For one thing," he continued, "I need your input on the investigation."

Her gasp of indignation had him scrambling to explain. "We both want to solve it, Marigold, and neither of us will be able to move on until we do."

"Okay, I see your point," she replied. "Whoever stole the Orcadol needs to be caught and punished before someone else gets hurt."

He swallowed hard, relieved that she agreed. The pressure on him to close the case was increasing, a PR nightmare, as well as a growing threat to the community. Part of his reason for taking today off had been to strengthen their working partnership, at least that was the argument he'd used on himself when he succumbed to the temptation of spending time with her.

He gestured with the hand he had extended and she had failed to grasp. "As far as this personal thing between us is concerned, maybe we should just see where it goes."

To him, the wording sounded like something Dr. Phil would have said. He smiled hopefully.

"This personal *thing?*" she echoed. "Is that what you'd call it?"

When he heard her tone, Bryce's smile faded. Oh, oh. Stepped in a cow pie.

"Frankly, I'm not sure what to call it. Getting involved again isn't something I planned, Marigold." The muscles of his throat tightened, making it harder for him to speak. "It felt right, that's all."

To his mingled surprise and relief, she finally slid her hand into his. "Then we just see where it leads, no strings and no expectations."

At least she hadn't said "no sex."

"Agreed," he said quickly, before she could change her mind. Miraculously, his headache seemed to have disappeared and he'd managed to extricate himself from the invitation to her grandmother's party.

What had she agreed to? Mari wondered a few moments later after Bryce had gone.

He had walked her to the door of her condo and waited for her to unlock it. Before she could thank him again and send him on his way, he dropped a couple of hints about hanging around and fixing a meal together. Because she needed space to sort out her feelings and time for chores she wouldn't get done tomorrow, she had ignored his hint. But before she could herd Bryce back outside, he took her into his arms and kissed her with a thoroughness that did serious damage to her resolve.

If it hadn't been for the look of male satisfaction

brimming in his gray eyes, she doubted she'd have found the strength to let him leave.

Blinking, Mari pulled herself back to the present. She checked the machine for messages, relieved that there was nothing that needed her urgent attention.

"Well," she said to Lennox as she sorted her laundry into piles, "I think I've agreed to keep sleeping with him and not expect anything more to come of it."

"Meow," Lennox replied, bottle-green eyes staring up at her intently.

"You're taking his side because he's a guy," Mari scolded, scooping laundry soap into the washing machine.

After she had started the cycle and added the sheets from her bed, she lowered her voice to a whisper.

"I'm afraid he's going to let me down again."

If she had expected a reaction from the cat, she was doomed to disappointment. The sound of the washing machine always made Lennox a little nervous. With a twitch of his ringed tail, he walked away as she closed the lid.

How was Bryce going to spend his Saturday night, she wondered. Since she'd turned him away, would he be on the prowl for other female companionship?

Bryce walked into the crowded roadhouse out on the highway and stood by the door. He let the loud music and the warm, stale air assault him as he looked around the crowded, dimly lit room for a familiar face.

The bartender, a part-time biker named Mark with a long gray ponytail, nodded silently as he filled a schooner from the tap. Behind Mark were rows of liquor bottles topped by a display of neon beer signs that glowed through the haze of secondhand smoke.

The dance floor was crowded, as were the tables surrounding it and the row of booths along one wall. Three men were seated at the bar. They checked Bryce out with nervous glances and one of them patted his shirt pocket furtively. Bryce ignored them all.

"Help you?" Mark called out above the rowdy George Jones song blaring from the sound system.

Bryce ordered a beer and paid for it. "Seen Joey?" he asked.

This was the third place he'd been in what was probably a pointless search for his brother. Joey could be anywhere, at someone's place getting drunk or high, or holed up alone. Their folks hadn't heard from him.

This wasn't really his crowd, but Bryce was too restless to sit at home twiddling his thumbs and Mari had kicked him out. Each time he thought they were getting closer, she took a step away.

Mark shook his head. "He hasn't been around in a couple of weeks." He motioned Bryce closer and lowered his voice. "What's up with him? He tried to run a tab, promised to pay when a big deal he's got in the works comes down."

"Did you let him?" Bryce asked.

Mark gave a crack of laughter. "You see 'stupid' tattooed on my forehead?" He glanced around. "Everyone here's waiting for the money train to pull in, but I ain't no bank."

"If you see him, tell him to call me," Bryce said.

Leaving the schooner untouched, he turned to go. A woman with curly blond hair walked up and blocked his way. When she tipped back her head, she looked vaguely familiar and a little bit drunk.

"Hi." She was fairly pretty and not too old. Her tight top barely covered a great pair of tits with nipples like hazelnuts. Her perfume tickled his nose. "All alone?" she asked.

Bryce wasn't on the clock, so he had the option of buying her a drink and maybe cuddling her close on the dance floor while he whispered in her ear. He could take her back to his place to grind Orchid, Mari and Joey out of his mind for a time.

Too bad he'd outgrown the appeal of casual sex years before. Without it, the kind of titillation the blonde was working seemed pretty pointless, too.

"Sorry, no," he replied with false regret. "Maybe next time."

Her shiny red lips flashed an answering smile that failed to reach her eyes. "I'll look for you," she said.

When she walked away, her low-cut pants showed off a butterfly tattoo and legs that went on for a mile. She wouldn't be alone for long.

With a last wistful glance, Bryce headed back to

his empty duplex so he could nurse a beer and brood alone. He'd go back over the Orchid case. There had to be something he was missing.

"How many people are we expecting this year?" Mari asked her grandmother as the two of them sat in the cream-and-beige living room, sipping iced tea with lemon and sprigs of mint.

"I didn't keep an exact count," was her grandmother's slightly defensive reply.

Myrtle Bingham usually preferred her own sitting room with its pink-and-red decor and her special chair, a throne on which no one else sat. Today the working fireplace made the room a little too warm.

As usual, what had started out as a simple family celebration had grown to a much larger event, thanks mostly to Myrtle herself. She adored parties and loved sharing the hospitality of her spacious home. Over the last few weeks, she had probably invited everyone she knew.

The rest of the family had all gone home from church to change their clothes. Mari had come early to help out.

The caterers had taken over the large kitchen, swarming like oversize ants. The florist was around back unloading her van. Outside the window, another crew was setting up tables, chairs and a canopy. Thanks to the gardeners' dedication, the flower beds were a work of art and the lawn looked like green velvet, despite the dry summer.

"It's your day," Mari said, patting her grandmother's hand. "You can invite whoever you please."

"I should think so," Myrtle replied with an audible sniff. The twinkle in her eye softened her tone and her rosy cheeks betrayed her excitement.

"You look very nice," Mari commented, helping herself to an ice-box cookie from the tray. "Is that a new outfit?"

"Nearly so. I bought it for a wedding shower in June."

Despite the casual tone of the party, Myrtle wore a tailored navy-blue shirt and slacks, a single strand of pearls and matching earrings. As always, her silver hair was freshly done, as were her nails and makeup.

Although she looked like a wealthy matron, Myrtle Bingham had been the driving force behind the establishment of the women's clinic, the hospital and the midwifery school. She had donated land for the library and the county rec center with its pool and other facilities. She'd encouraged her late husband to provide scholarships and charitable foundations, doing her best to offset some of the townspeople's animosity toward her family.

Ever since she had arrived from Boston as a new bride, she had worked hard to make a place for herself here. There was no one Mari respected more. Her grandmother was the biggest reason she was so determined to build the research center and carry on the legacy of providing the best health care possible for the women of Kentucky.

"You look especially attractive today, my dear." Myrtle studied her carefully. "There's a glow to your skin and a sparkle in your eyes that I've missed seeing. Have you met someone new?"

Mari's cheeks heated. Trust her grandmother to notice!

"Afraid not." Technically it wasn't a lie, since Bryce had been in her life before.

Her grandmother took a sip of tea, her hand shaking slightly. She frowned at Mari over the top of her glass, obviously disappointed.

"So you won't be bringing anyone today?"

Nervously Mari pushed the half-eaten cookie around on her plate. She had been dying to talk about Bryce, even though she couldn't tell her grandmother *everything,* of course.

"Actually I did invite a guest," she confessed.

Her grandmother perked up immediately. "Really? Is it someone I know?"

At seventy-eight, she wasn't as active as she'd been in the past, but she still attended hospital board meetings, so she was acquainted with many staff members there and at the clinic.

Suddenly Mari realized that her grandmother might have actually met the person stealing Orcadol. It was a chilling thought.

"Marigold?" Myrtle asked.

Mari blinked and refocused. "I'm sorry. I was just thinking about a problem at work."

"Anything I can help with, my dear?"

"No, thank you. It's just a personnel problem." What an understatement!

"So tell me," her grandmother persisted. "Who's the young man you've invited to join us today?" She smiled expectantly.

Oh dear. Mari hadn't meant to raise her expectations.

"I'm sorry," she confessed. "I said that I asked someone, but it turns out he couldn't make it after all."

Her grandmother tipped her head to the side like a bird. "Am I to know the name of this simpleton who didn't have the sense to accept?" Her voice had sharpened considerably, her gaze intent.

Mari fought the urge to squirm, wishing she'd kept her big mouth shut.

"It's Bryce," she mumbled as she toyed with her iced-tea spoon. "Bryce Collins. Do you remember him?"

"Marigold, that's not at all funny. Detective Collins is the one trying to blame you for the missing drugs." Her grandmother's voice had chilled considerably.

Even after all these years, that tone could still make Mari quake in her shoes. Or her sandals, which she had on today with her favorite pastel plaid sundress.

Resigned, she met her grandmother's piercing stare.

"I'm not kidding. I really did invite him." She took a deep breath. "It's a long story and I shouldn't have brought it up on your birthday."

Desperate for a diversion, Mari glanced at the present she'd set on the sideboard. This morning she had wrapped it in sunflower-covered paper, all the while wishing Bryce would call.

"What's troubling you, child?" Her grandmother rested her clasped hands on the table and waited patiently.

Mari gulped back sudden tears. Unburdening herself to her grandmother was always a relief, but it wouldn't be fair to do so now. Not when the other guests were due to begin arriving at any time.

"I've been working too much," she said. "And I guess I haven't been sleeping well."

"What's wearing you down is that damned investigation and someone's ridiculous idea that you could be involved."

Mari was surprised to hear her grandmother use such language. She was a lady to her toes, but under the pampered skin was a will of iron and a mind that age hadn't yet dulled.

"Unofficially, I'm no longer a suspect," Mari said, "even though we haven't found the real criminal yet."

"We?" her grandmother echoed. "What exactly is going on between you and that detective?"

"I'm helping Bryce with the investigation," she said softly. "I have a stake in it, too, you know."

Before either of them could say more, Mari's brother, Geoff, and his bride came into the room.

"My three favorite women, all in one place," Geoff said with an expansive wave of his arm.

Once the ultimate Type-A business tycoon, Geoff had obviously found a sense of balance in his relationship with Eric Mendoza's sister. Before Geoff and Cecilia's elopement, a suit and tie had been his customary attire, no matter the occasion. Today he wore cutoff jeans and a Hawaiian shirt in vibrant colors, topped by a relaxed and happy grin.

As Mari slid back her chair, he bent down and gave Myrtle a kiss on the cheek. "Happy birthday, Grandma."

Mari hugged Cecilia and then she turned to Geoff while their grandmother rose to greet his wife. More people began to arrive. Greetings were exchanged and gifts set on the table. With the graciousness of someone who genuinely loved people and the ease of a born hostess, Myrtle led them all outside.

The caterers, Mari noticed, had set up a long table under the canopy. Flowers and balloons were everywhere. As more guests arrived, cold drinks and food were being dispensed with smiling efficiency. Myrtle was having a ball as the numbers swelled.

"Just a small Bingham family party," Kyle said softly from behind Mari.

She turned to see him with Milla and Dylan.

"I'm so glad you came!" Mari exclaimed, arms

outstretched. She embraced first Milla, whose radiance nearly brought tears to Mari's eyes, and then Kyle. She knew better than to hug Dylan, who was watching her approach with obvious alarm.

"Don't worry," Mari assured him. "No PDAs. How are you?"

"Fine, thank you," he responded politely. "Can I get some soda?" he asked Milla.

"No what, PDAs?" Kyle asked after Dylan had left for the food table.

"Public displays of affection," Mari replied. "The kiss of death to a nine-year-old, I'm sure."

"Something he'll outgrow soon enough," Kyle replied. "Probably when puberty hits."

Mari noticed her father arriving with Lily. The two of them were holding hands.

"Would you excuse me?" she asked Milla and Kyle. "Have something to eat and I'll catch up with you later."

"Sure thing," Kyle replied. "We haven't said hello to Grandma yet."

Mari's father had been widowed for a decade by the time her good friend, Lily, came to town in response to Mari's plea for help raising funds for the research center. She knew her father suspected her of matchmaking, but Lily and her mother were as different as two women could be.

Mari had begun to suspect that Lily and her father were having a discreet affair. Before they met, he had started to cut back on his responsibilities at work with the idea of helping Mari get the research project off the drawing board. In his spare time, he took up gardening, but his restlessness soon became obvious. When he admitted to Mari that he had found love a second time in his life, afraid she would think him disloyal to her mother, she had been thrilled. He and Lily were a good match.

"Hey, you two," Mari called out as they walked toward her across the lawn. "How are you?"

Her father, still handsome and trim in his fifties, released Lily's hand long enough to wrap his arms around Mari. His neat gray beard rubbed her cheek.

"How's my best girl holding up?" he asked into her ear.

Mari patted his back. "I'm fine, Dad. It always lifts my spirits to see you so happy."

Stepping back, she exchanged a brush of cheeks and air kisses with Lily, whose work raising money for inner-city mothers had first brought her to Mari's attention. The two of them had become friends before Mari hired her as the PR director for the clinic.

Mari was one of the few people who knew that Lily's first marriage had failed because of her inability to have children. As a hugely successful fundraiser and public-relations expert, Lily had traveled the world. Since she'd come to Merlyn County, though, she insisted that she had found both her home and her soul mate.

Lily searched Mari's face intently before letting go

of her hand. "How are you really holding up, sweetie?"

Mari gave her a big smile. Today wasn't the time for serious conversations.

"Pretty well." She saw her grandmother talking to two of her elderly friends. "Doesn't Grandma look great?"

Lily took the hint. "Wait till you see the pajamas we bought her." She rolled her eyes. "Black silk with lace trim and a robe to match. I can't wait to see her expression when she opens them."

"She'll probably cut us out of her will," Mari's father grumbled, but he didn't appear too concerned.

"She'll love them," Mari assured them both with a chuckle. Myrtle might be from a different generation, but she was very open-minded. "Have something to eat and I'll see you later."

"I want to hear about the conference at UK," her father reminded her. "And the reception."

Mari recalled that she'd hoped to meet the wealthy couple who hadn't shown up. Her father would be disappointed to hear that, but between the two of them, he and Lily had many more contacts. In time, the center would become a reality.

Mari was a little surprised to see three of the nurses who worked at the hospital, although she shouldn't have been. Her grandma's hospitality cast a wide net and she was well known at the medical complex.

The nurses were sitting together at a table with plates of food from the buffet. Two were dressed for work in pastel uniform smocks and slacks, the other, Crystal Hendrix, wore shorts and a halter top.

It was nice to see her getting out, even though she didn't appear to be eating. Instead she sipped from a tall glass of cola while she fiddled with the locket she wore around her neck. The petite blonde was already thin. If she wasn't careful, she'd lose too much weight.

Crystal's little boy, Ryan, was off somewhere visiting his father. She was a young single mother and the separation seemed to be very difficult for her. At work she had been nervous and preoccupied, to the point where Mari had had no choice but to speak to her once already. Mari made a mental note to ask when Ryan was coming home. The school year had already started, so it must be soon. Good nurses were difficult to find and Mari hated letting anyone go. She was hoping Crystal would settle down once he was back.

"Hey, Mari, look who we brought." Once again, Eric Mendoza was proudly showing off Hannah's tiny baby girl, asleep in her carrier. Hannah, looking lovely, was standing beside him.

"Hello, Dr. Bingham," she said shyly.

"Hannah, we're family," Mari exclaimed. "Please don't be so formal. Hi, Eric. I'll miss seeing your smiling face at the meetings with the hospital, but it looks like you've found something a lot more fun."

Technically he wasn't the baby's father, but one would never know that from the way he'd been bragging and carrying on ever since Mari's cousin had given birth.

Mari bent down for a closer look.

"Can I pick her up?" she asked.

"Of course," Hannah replied. "I'm sure you know what you're doing."

Her teasing comment surprised a laugh from Mari. Gently she scooped up the infant, cute as a bug in a one-piece romper and a tiny ruffled hat, and cuddled her in the crook of one arm. The baby's face scrunched into a frown, and she moved her tiny mouth.

No matter how many babies Mari delivered, a feeling of awe welled up inside her every time she held one. Someday she hoped to have a child of her own.

"She's a doll," she said sincerely. "You're so lucky."

"I know." Eric slid his arm around Hannah's waist and she rested her blond head against his shoulder. Their obvious devotion sent a shiver of envy through Mari.

Suddenly she realized how much she would love to have Bryce's baby. The more time she spent with him, the more she realized that he had the character traits she would want in a spouse. Shocked, Mari nearly dropped the infant she was holding!

Luckily, neither Eric nor Hannah seemed to notice. When she looked up at him, he seemed to give her a nod of encouragement.

"Um, there's something we wanted to ask you,"

Hannah said once Mari had settled the baby back into her carrier and pulled up the light covering.

"What's that?" she asked, straightening.

"Would you be willing to be our baby's god-mother?" Hannah asked in a rush.

Mari's gaze went from Hannah's blushing face to Eric's. In his job as the hospital director, he was well aware of the problems with Orcadol and the rumors about Mari. He couldn't have already heard, though, about the forged prescriptions.

"Are you sure?" she asked, extremely moved by their request.

The couple seemed able to read the direction of her thoughts. Eric grinned and Hannah touched Mari's arm gently.

"There isn't anyone else who could set a better example of character, devotion and service to others," she told Mari. "We'd be honored."

Tears filled Mari's eyes, and she had to blink quickly to keep them from spilling over.

"Thank you," Mari whispered. "I'm the one who's honored."

As if on cue, the baby girl opened her eyes and began to fuss. It was amazing how much noise could come from such a small package.

"Feeding time," Hannah said, glancing around.

"Why don't you take her into the house," Mari suggested. "You'll be more comfortable."

"Thanks. We'll talk again soon," Eric said.

After they'd walked away, Mari decided she had

better get something to eat before Myrtle started opening the presents that someone had brought outside. Mari was feeling a little wrung out emotionally, especially since her conversation with the Mendozas and her realization about Bryce.

She grabbed a plate and filled it without paying a lot of attention to what she was taking. With it in one hand and a glass of lemonade in the other, she looked around for an empty chair.

An arm shot up and her brother waved her over to where he was sitting with their father, Cecilia and Lily. When Mari approached the table, Geoff got to his feet and held out her chair.

"I'm glad to see you eating something," he said after she'd thanked him. "You've lost too much weight."

"You never tell *me* that," Cecilia teased as Mari dug into her potato salad.

Cecilia had recently confided that she was expecting their first child. Since the dark-haired beauty was a few years older than Geoff, Mari could understand their desire to start a family right away.

"I love you the way you are," Geoff replied gallantly. "And I'll love you even more when you're nine months along."

"Well put, son," their father said, clapping Geoff on the back. "How are you feeling?" he asked Cecilia.

"A little tired," she replied, "but I expect that will pass eventually."

Mari concentrated on her plate, forking up bites of chicken salad, slaw and a square of something pink that quivered when Lily bumped the table.

"I saw Bryce Collins at the bank the other day," Geoff said unexpectedly. "It was all I could do not to walk up and punch him in the nose."

"Why?" Mari blurted without thinking. "The poor man is just doing his job."

The other four occupants at the table all stared, making her realize that she'd been a little too adamant in her defense. Perhaps it was just as well that Bryce had turned down her invitation. She'd forgotten how strongly Geoff resented him.

Her brother had always blamed Bryce for breaking her heart when she was young. Now the investigation had only served to strengthen Geoff's dislike.

"She's right," their father said unexpectedly. "Detective Collins is doing his job."

"Dad! What are you saying?" With his cheeks flushing a dusky red, Geoff gaped as though Ron had lost his mind. "The bastard has been trying to railroad Mari into jail just to advance his own career."

"That's not exactly true," she mumbled. "There was some evidence that pointed him in my direction."

To her surprise, Geoff pushed back his chair and got to his feet.

"I don't believe what I'm hearing." He glanced at Cecilia. "I'm going to find myself a cold beer. Do you want something?"

"No thanks, honey." She turned to Lily. "Shall we powder our noses?" she asked pointedly.

"What is this?" Mari demanded as both women stood up. "A conspiracy?"

Her father attempted to look innocent, failing utterly. "Don't ask me."

Once again Mari marveled at the change in his appearance since he'd met Lily. He looked more relaxed and he'd lost the air of loneliness she had always sensed lurking beneath his smile.

"Are you okay?" he asked, his smile fading as the other two women left. "Tell me the truth. I'm concerned about you and so is your grandmother."

Something clutched at Mari's throat. "Did she say something to you today?"

"Not specifically, why?" He looked puzzled. "Is there something going on I should know about?" His chuckle lacked humor. "I mean, something more than what you're already going through."

With his extremely busy schedule, her father hadn't always had the time to be an understanding parent, but he'd tried. Mari had known without doubt that he loved her mother with all his heart and that he loved his children, too.

"I've been helping Bryce with the investigation," she admitted, just as she had told her grandmother. And, like Myrtle, her father's expression registered disbelief.

"Why would you do that?" he asked. "You don't know anything about police work."

"But I know my employees," she replied, "and it's pretty obvious that one of them is responsible for stealing Orcadol from the clinic."

She hated saying it out loud, as though speaking the words made them true. She hadn't been ready to face reality, but there was no other reasonable explanation.

"Is it difficult for you to be around him?" her father asked.

"Only when he's trying to arrest me," she quipped.

She hadn't confided in her father when she and Bryce broke up, but he had been able to tell that something was wrong. On one occasion when she was back from school for the weekend, her father had mentioned at dinner in front of Myrtle and Geoff that he'd seen Bryce around town. He had then asked, with a male's simple lack of awareness of the undercurrents swirling around him, whether Mari was going to visit Bryce while she was home.

She'd bolted from the table in a storm of tears, and Geoff told her later with a grin that Myrtle had called their father an idiot. That made a far bigger impression on her younger brother than her tears ever could.

"Is there anything I can do?" her father asked now. "You know that I wanted to hire you an attorney when this business all started."

"I know." She patted his hand. "It's beginning to look as though paying someone a big retainer would have been a real waste of money."

"Helping out my daughter is never a waste," he replied without a moment's pause. "You know I'd do anything for you or Geoff."

He glanced at Lily, walking back across the lawn with Cecilia. "Even though she's never been a parent, Lily understands that."

"She would make a wonderful mother," Mari said softly.

The caterer, a plump older woman, came over to their table. With a polite nod to Mari, she leaned down to speak to Ron.

"Excuse me, but you asked me to let you know when it was time to cut the cake. Everyone appears to have finished eating, so what do you think?"

"Thank you, Loretta." He set aside his napkin. "The food was wonderful, as usual."

He had helped her start her business with a loan she had since repaid. Loretta still catered every Bingham event.

Her weathered cheeks turned pink. "I'm glad you enjoyed it."

"Who made the cake?" Mari asked. "It's very clever."

The birthday cake, a full sheet, was decorated like a giant bingo card. Although Myrtle always insisted that games of chance were time wasters and that gambling was the devil's nonsense, she played bingo nearly every week in the church basement.

"Rose Henderson does our decorating," Loretta replied. "She's got five kids, so she likes working part-time.'' She tucked a strand of hair behind her ear. ''I'll pass on what you said.''

Mari's father slid back his chair. ''Would you see that the champagne is served?'' he asked Loretta. ''Mari, you let me know if you need anything. Meanwhile, I'd better go make the toast.''

Chapter Nine

"Sheriff Remington wants to see you ASAP."

Christine didn't bother to hide her smirk as she gave Bryce the news. Speaking around the gum she chewed, she made sure that her voice carried to everyone in the squad room. There was a rumor circulating that she had been seen parked in a patrol car with a deputy who was newly separated from his wife. Whether or not that was true, Christine must still have resented Bryce for his lack of interest.

"Thanks." His stomach had taken a sudden dive at the news, but he managed a smile that revealed nothing.

Frowning, she spun back to her computer with a

huff of disappointment. Bryce had the Orcadol file with him, so he crossed the room and stuck his head through the partly opened doorway to the sheriff's office.

"You wanted to see me, Sheriff?"

Sheriff Remington glanced up at Bryce. He wasn't smiling, which was always a bad sign. He was a stickler for proper procedure, and he had worked his way up through the ranks. Bryce had found him to be tough, but fair.

"Close the door, Detective, and sit down."

Laying the folder on his knees, Bryce took the hot seat. He tried not to squirm like a truant schoolboy in the principal's office as the sheriff's gaze raked over him.

The silence lengthened. Other deputies had admitted, after a few beers, to cracking under pressure, but Bryce was prepared. He had thoroughly reviewed the case last night after getting home.

The sheriff drummed his fingers on the desktop. "Normally I don't get involved in my staff's personal lives."

"Yes, sir." It took Bryce a moment to switch gears and then he swallowed hard. He should have seen this coming. There wasn't anything the sheriff didn't know about his deputies and detectives.

"It's come to my attention that you've been seen in the company of a certain doctor you're supposed to be investigating." Bryce's boss appeared deeply disappointed. It was much more effective than anger.

Bryce knew better than to argue, but the words came out before he could stop them.

"Sheriff, you told me yourself that the handwriting on the script we found wasn't Dr. Bingham's."

Sheriff Remington's thick white brows rose above his icy-blue eyes. "And how is this relevant?"

Since Bryce had opened his big fat mouth and confirmed the situation, he had no choice but to proceed.

"I needed Mari's cooperation to view the employee files at the clinic, but she wouldn't release them to me. In order to save time, we ended up going through them together."

A trickle of sweat inched its way down his back, but he ignored it.

"Are you telling me that was the extent of your contact with *Mari?*"

Bryce had no idea how much the sheriff knew, but he recognized a snare when he was about to step into one. Lying would get him bounced back to street patrol for sure.

"No, sir." He was gripping the file folder so hard that it bent. Carefully he loosened his fingers.

The sheriff sighed and leaned back in his heavy leather chair. It squeaked in protest as he glanced pointedly at the folder.

"Bring me up to speed on the Orcadol case."

"Yes, sir." Bryce cleared his throat, nervous as a rookie. "The clinic does its own background checks on everyone it hires. I've been running additional checks on the employees with access to the drug cabinet, but so far nothing has come up.''

"And we're not overworking you?'' the sheriff asked. "You're able to take your scheduled time off, to get away?''

That's how he'd been busted, Bryce realized. Someone had seen him and Mari on Saturday. It could have been worse.

"Yes, sir. Thank you for asking, sir.''

The corner of the sheriff's mouth twitched and was instantly stilled.

"You wouldn't be rash enough to jerk my chain, would you, Detective?''

Bryce stiffened. "No, Sheriff.''

Sheriff Remington sat forward, steepling his fingers beneath his square chin. "Did you see the unflattering cartoon of me in Sunday's *Mage*? Pretty clever, really.''

Bryce knew better than to agree or to blink or even to breathe when the sheriff's reputation was involved.

"You've got forty-eight hours to bring me something solid, or I'm taking you off the case.'' He leaned down and opened a file drawer. "Leave the door open. It gets too damned hot in here with it shut.''

"Thank you, Sheriff,'' Bryce mumbled, nearly dropping the folder when he got to his feet. If he didn't figure this out fast, the case would be reassigned to Hank Butler.

For Mari's sake, as well as his own, Bryce couldn't let that happen.

For the last quarter hour, Mari had been sitting in her office staring out the window. She ignored the pile of work on her desk, preferring instead to mentally review her grandmother's birthday party.

Dad's toast had been touching and Myrtle got some lovely gifts. She especially seemed to appreciate the black silk pajamas and Mari's honeysuckle-scented soap.

The bingo-themed cake was also a big hit. After she blew out the candles, it had been cut and consumed. A short time later, everyone drifted away.

Mari could see that her grandmother was getting tired. The caterer's crew seemed to have the cleanup under control, so she didn't linger, even though she would have liked to ask Myrtle's advice.

Perhaps Bryce had been smart to refuse Mari's invitation. Myrtle would never have allowed a guest to be treated with anything less than courtesy, but he probably would have been wearing a chip on his broad shoulder. Although Geoff would never have been disrespectful enough to start anything, neither would he have bothered to hide his dislike. How many other people would have made Bryce feel unwelcome, especially those who'd known Mari long enough to remember the painful breakup?

She began looking through the stack of messages she hadn't felt like dealing with earlier when her intercom buzzed. She glanced up at the wall clock, amazed to see that she'd had more than twenty uninterrupted minutes.

"Yes?" she asked, leaning forward.

"Do you have time for Detective Collins?" asked the disembodied voice.

Tension curling in her stomach, Mari reached for the phone. She and Bryce hadn't parted on the friendliest of terms on Saturday.

"Which line?" she asked.

"He's here at the desk. Shall I send him along?"

Here? Automatically, Mari's hand groped for the small mirror that she kept in her drawer. Stopping herself, she pushed back her chair.

"No need, Heather. I'll come out."

When she saw him leaning against the counter talking to the receptionist, Mari's heart skipped a couple of beats. It quickened into double time when he looked up, just as though he had sensed her approach.

He leaned back down to say something to Heather, who laughed appreciatively.

Bryce straightened away from the counter and his gaze met hers. Once again she felt a zing of awareness shoot through her.

"Detective," she said calmly. "What can I do for you?"

Something glinted in his eyes and was quickly doused, but the expression on his chiseled face remained serious.

"Is there somewhere we can talk?" he asked politely.

Oh, she knew where this was going! If he thought for one second that they were having another rendezvous in her office—especially while the clinic was open—he was dead wrong.

She was proud of the cool smile she managed to produce. "Of course. I was just about to go over to the cafeteria for something to eat. Would you like to join me?"

If he was disappointed by her suggestion, he kept the emotion hidden.

"I'd like that," he said, sliding his hands into the pockets of his tan slacks. "Are you buying?"

Heather, who had been openly eavesdropping on their exchange, did a poor job of muffling her chuckle. Ducking her head to avoid Mari's icy glance, she became intent on her computer screen.

"Don't you public servants have an expense account for meals?" Mari shot back at Bryce.

He didn't bother to hide the humor dancing in his eyes. "Does this mean we're going dutch?" he asked.

Mari turned away from the counter. How dare he act as though everything were peachy between them. She still hadn't figured out to what convoluted male pact she'd agreed.

"It's not a date," she hissed as she headed for the sky bridge.

"It never is," he sighed.

Effortlessly his long-legged strides caught up to her

so he could lean closer. ''I guess that means no goodbye kiss in your office,'' he added in a husky whisper.

She wanted to stop in the middle of the walkway
and demand to know what he thought he was doing.
No, what she really, really wanted was to haul back
her arm and clobber him. To do either would draw
unwanted attention to the two of them, so she quickened her pace instead. He was forced to drop back to
pass an orderly pushing a woman in a wheelchair.

Neither Mari nor Bryce spoke again until he sat
down across from her at a table in the cafeteria. Not
surprisingly, her appetite had fled.

Resentfully she watched Bryce unload his tray.
When he was done, he set it on the next table and
then he looked from his heaping plate of pasta with
meatballs and cheese toast to her green salad.

''No wonder you're getting skinny.''

Bristling, she picked up her fork and poked at the
greens she no longer wanted.

''You, on the other hand, are headed for a heart
attack,'' she said. ''What's your cholesterol level?''

He leaned forward. ''I love it when you go all doctor on me. Say something else in medical lingo.''

If she hadn't been so annoyed with him, she would
have laughed out loud at his pleading expression. Instead she drizzled poppy-seed dressing over her salad.
Before she took a bite, she glanced around the half-
empty room.

Two women who had been watching them looked

quickly away. One of them leaned across the table to whisper something and they both laughed.

To a stranger, Mari and Bryce might look like just any other couple sharing a meal. However, most of the locals would recognize one or both of them and wonder what they could possibly have to discuss without one of those dreadfully bright interrogation lights shining down on Mari.

"How was the party?" Bryce asked after he had chewed and swallowed some of the pasta.

"Everyone seemed to have a great time," she replied. "Too bad you couldn't make it."

His gaze remained steady on hers while he broke off a piece of bread. "I don't think your family is quite ready to accept me on a social level."

She recalled Geoff's attitude. Perhaps Bryce was right, but how her family might feel about him wasn't something that was ever likely to be tested.

"I'm not Joey's favorite person, either," she had to point out.

"I guess it would be a small wedding," he drawled. "Think of the money we'd save."

She had no idea what to say to that. "Why did you want to see me?" she asked.

"Do I need a reason?" His voice was unexpectedly soft.

She had to swallow hard as a wave of longing washed over her. Why couldn't life be simple and straightforward, like science?

"I had a nice time on Saturday," she admitted, surprising herself.

"Me, too." His reply shocked her even more.

For a moment, his face looked unbearably sad. Then he swallowed and glanced away.

"There's been a complication."

Mari was puzzled. Their relationship, if what they had together could be called that, was full of complications.

"What do you mean?" she asked carefully.

"Someone must have seen us together on Saturday. We've been ratted out to Sheriff Remington. He called me into his office first thing this morning to remind me that he's not happy with my lack of progress. Now he's got a reason to yank me off the case."

Fear grabbed her heart and brought tears to her eyes, making her realize how much she had come to count on Bryce.

"Who took over for you?"

"No one yet. He's given me a couple of days to come up with something solid, but I wanted you to know what's going on."

Clearing his throat, he leaned toward her across the table. "I shouldn't be saying this, but it may be time for you to consult an attorney. I'm sure your family can find you a good one."

She took a deep breath. "They've been pressuring me to do just that, but I refuse to allow people to get the impression that I'm trying to hide something. My professional reputation is too important to me.''

''I understand,'' he replied, ''but the system isn't perfect. Sometimes innocent people get run down by those wheels of justice we keep hearing about.''

He was obviously trying to warn her. ''What can we do?'' she asked.

He swirled the pasta around on his plate. ''If there's any bit of information you've held back from me, anything you didn't think was important or anyone you've been protecting, you've got to come clean with me now.'' His eyes narrowed, reminding her that first and foremost he was a detective trying to solve a case. ''Think hard.''

His remark was probably aimed at Ricardo, but she refused to believe that her colleague could be involved. Besides, there was no way he could have switched the pills at the clinic. He didn't have access.

She stared down at her salad but found no answers in the wilting greens. Discouraged, she shook her head.

''There's nothing you don't already know.'' Head bowed, she struggled for control. ''Is this ever going to end?'' she whispered, half to herself.

Bryce made a low sound in his throat. ''Mari, look at me.'' His voice was sharp.

When she complied, gritting her teeth to keep her chin from wobbling, she was surprised by his determined expression.

"I know you're innocent," he said. "And I've got two days to figure out how to prove it."

His words caused a wave of relief to well up in her throat. "Thank you for saying that," she choked.

"Oh, jeez. Don't get all female on me now," he exclaimed, drawing back from her as though she had been chewing garlic.

Like a splash of cold water, his comment jerked her back to reality. It was probably just what he had intended.

As much as she had tried to ignore his existence through the years, she'd heard comments about him. A while back, the *Mage* had printed a brief profile on him as part of a series about local careers. He was said to be fair and fierce, unrelenting in his pursuit of criminals. Once she had overheard a couple of EMTs talking, and one made the comment that Bryce was squeaky clean.

She didn't figure he'd been referring to Bryce's personal hygiene.

Suddenly everything fell into place and a feeling of peace dissolved the knot in her stomach. When she looked back up, she was able to smile as she reached out to pat the hand he'd curled into a fist.

"I trust you," she said with conviction. "Now trust yourself and get busy."

He didn't appear pleased by her reply. "Didn't you hear what I said about the sheriff? I'm running out of time."

"Okay. What's next?" she asked, determined to

hang on to the belief that everything was going to work out. Maybe once the two of them had put this behind them, they could even spend some more one-on-one time together.

The idea made her blush. Thank goodness Bryce couldn't read her mind.

"I'm going to go back over the notes I took on your employment files," he said with a determined frown as he pushed away the half-eaten plate of food and got to his feet. "I've got a gut feeling that there's something right in front of me that I'm just not seeing."

If Marigold's intention had been to totally distract Bryce from his work, she had done a bang-up job. Ever since he'd left her at the hospital and returned to the office, he'd had a devil of a time staying focused on the task at hand.

What he had viewed as a straightforward desire to get her back into bed had suddenly gotten complicated. He wanted more from her than sex, but he had no idea whether they could put the past behind them, where it belonged, in order to explore possible options for the future.

His brother held her family personally accountable for the accident that had crippled their father. Mari's family obviously resented Bryce for hurting her in the past, as well as for the drug investigation that focused on her as the main person of interest.

With that much baggage between them, did the two

of them stand a snowball's chance in a Kentucky summer of building a future together? Could he trust her with his heart a second time?

Since the sheriff had left a little while ago to attend a luncheon meeting with the county council and wasn't expected back today, Christine had taken the opportunity to crank up the rap music on her CD player to an annoying level. A rookie waiting for his shift to start was keeping time with his nightstick.

Finally, Bryce tossed down his pencil and rubbed his aching temples with his fingertips. No matter what he decided to do about his escalating feelings for Mari, his first priority had to be busting the Orcadol ring. If Hank Butler took over the case, his habitual bungling and lazy police work might land Mari in jail while the real perps went free.

With painstaking thoroughness, Bryce dug out everything he had on the case and began to review it for what must have been the hundredth time. The first red flag had been the marked increase in the number of drug-addicted women giving birth at the Foster Clinic. At the same time, an informant had reported a rise in the supply of illegal Orchid on the streets, leading Bryce to begin looking for a connection between the two things.

"I'm making a burger run," announced a PA who had been filing documents. "Anyone got a craving?"

Bryce shook his head. "Thanks anyway."

He got up to refill his coffee mug with sludge. As he walked back to his desk, he recalled the woman who had come into the clinic demanding Orcadol while he was attempting to question Mari for the first time. Mari swore to him that the woman couldn't have gotten the drug from the clinic, but the incident had never been explained to his satisfaction. Neither had the prescription papers from Mari's pad that turned up during the raid at the dealer's.

A young mother had died of an Orcadol overdose and her child barely survived. As he read the report, he sipped the oily brew in his mug, hardly noticing its gut-churning taste.

Mari had also admitted that at least one patient who'd been prescribed Orcadol had been given something else accidentally, causing an allergic reaction. That had led Mari to have the drug tested at an independent lab. A different painkiller with a similar appearance had been substituted for some of the Orcadol in the supply cabinet. She had interviewed the staff, but—no surprise—had found out nothing useful.

He set down his mug and rotated his shoulders, which were getting stiff. For all the progress he was making, he could have gone to the gym to work out instead. Perhaps he would still do that when he finished up. At least lifting weights or a hard game of handball would help work off some of his frustration.

His thoughts strayed to Mari and another physical activity that could accomplish the same thing. Ignoring the wall clock, whose hands were moving too damned fast in sweeping away the time he had left, he proceeded to the list of clinic employees with access to the locked drug cabinet.

Perhaps he'd have to persuade Mari to give him another look at the files. She had a full schedule this afternoon, but she'd promised to be available by phone if anything came up.

His gaze ran down the alphabetical list of names. He had gone over it so many times that he could have recited it from memory.

As he forced his gaze to move slowly, one name caught his attention. Crystal Hendrix. Why did it have a familiar ring?

Frowning, he dug out the rest of his information on Crystal. *Crystal.* He could hear his brother's voice as he bragged about a girl named Crystal. The name wasn't that common. When had the conversation with Joey taken place?

Bryce closed his eyes and concentrated. They didn't talk that often and it hadn't been the last time, so it wasn't hard to think back.

Bryce had been watching the basketball playoffs and Joey was drunk when he called. Bryce had had twenty bucks on the outcome of the final game, so he hadn't paid much attention to Joey's rambling about his new woman or his latest wild plan to bring down the Binghams. His slurred voice was difficult to understand, his idle threats easy to ignore, at the time.

What had the girl's name been? Crystal...Crystal what?

Suddenly Bryce could hear Joey's giggled words

in his head. Crystal *Hendrix,* same name as that rock guitarist who died. Yes!

Bryce sat up straight, nearly spilling his coffee, as he remembered his brother's sneering comment that she worked with Bryce's ex-witch. At the time he hadn't wanted to hear *anything* about Mari, good or bad. Now he wished he'd encouraged Joey to tell him more.

A surge of adrenaline made Bryce's hands shake as he sorted through the papers in front of him until he found her address. Was this the connection he'd been seeking?

Abruptly his elation evaporated. Joey was his only brother, the little kid Bryce had promised their parents he would look out for and protect. How could he suspect, for even a second, that his own flesh and blood might be involved?

It was true that Joey had problems—immaturity, a fondness for booze and partying, the inability to take responsibility for his actions or to hold down a job. He blamed others for everything that went wrong in his life. Had his twisted desire for revenge grown so strong that he would sink to stealing and selling drugs that ruined people's lives? Or was Bryce so blinded by hormones and so desperate to help Mari that he saw connections where none existed?

A new thought hit with the force of a truck. Did he want to clear Mari so badly that he would rather his own brother be guilty?

He nearly groaned aloud, forgetting for an instant

where he was. Shaken, he squeezed his eyes shut. Thank God the choice wasn't his to make.

He glanced down at Crystal's address again. If there was a connection between her, Joey and the stolen drugs, it was Bryce's sworn duty to find it.

Before he did, though, he'd try one more time to contact his brother. Not even to save him was Bryce willing to compromise either his principles or the investigation, but he hoped to get some idea of what, if anything, Joey might know about Crystal or Orchid.

Getting to his feet, Bryce dug his brother's latest cell-phone number out of his wallet and sent up a silent prayer that it was still good. He didn't dare risk calling from inside the squad, where he might be overheard.

Casually he walked outside to his car, parked in the shade of the building, and called on his cell. Joey didn't answer, so Bryce left a message. When he was through, he looked at his watch. If he didn't hear back in an hour, then he'd pay Ms. Hendrix a visit.

He toyed with the idea of going by Mari's while he waited, but he couldn't very well question Joey in her presence if he did call. Bryce didn't want her or anyone else to know the direction of his traitorous thoughts until he had something more concrete to go on.

He sat in his car, drumming his fingers on the wheel as he gazed through the windshield without seeing a thing. Suddenly his stomach rumbled a re-

minder that he hadn't eaten since the hospital cafeteria spaghetti and that had been hours ago.

He had two choices, to sit here and brood about
Mari or to get something to eat. Brooding about her
left him frustrated, but he had time for a burger before
Joey's hour was up.

The last person Mari expected to see when she
gave in to her craving and drove downtown for an
order of fish and chips was Bryce. He was sitting
outside South Junction Burgers in his unmarked department sedan. After ascertaining that he was alone,
she pulled up beside him.

He looked surprised and not especially pleased to
see her car. Was he on some kind of stakeout? The
last thing she wanted to do was blow his cover, but
she couldn't fight the surge of physical attraction she
felt whenever she was around him.

"Hungry?" he called through his open window as
she stood on shaky legs and walked around the front
of her car.

How would he react if she leaned down and planted
a big kiss on that luscious male mouth?

"Starving," she replied truthfully.

Good thing he couldn't read what was going
through her mind, or he might roll up his window and
lock his door!

His eyes narrowed. Was she drooling?

"I'll buy you a burger," he offered.

If she didn't bite into something, she was going to start nibbling on him.

"Make it fish and chips, and you've got a deal," she replied, voice husky.

"Whatever you want." He set his foil-wrapped burger up on the dash and started to open his door.

"No, don't get out." She needed a minute away from him to collect herself. "Finish your meal. You can reimburse me later."

His eyebrows rose, but he didn't say anything.

Mari sucked in a breath and leaned down so they were nearly nose to nose. "I'm talking cash, Collins, in case you were wondering," she taunted, her hands gripping the car door to keep herself from thrusting her fingers into his hair. "Get your mind out of the gutter."

To her disappointment, his lips barely twitched in response to her teasing.

"I'm waiting for a call, so I may have to leave," he said.

Mari sobered instantly. "What's going on?"

"Nothing you need to worry about." He picked up a fat hand-cut french fry and dipped it into a small container of ketchup.

An arguing couple with two kids walked by the car, drawing his attention.

Nibbling her lip, Mari studied his profile while he chewed nonchalantly. Something was up, she could feel it.

"Aren't you going to order?" he asked.

Between the waves of lust and curiosity, Mari's appetite had fled for the second time that day. Sneaking glances at Bryce through the front window, she went inside and waited impatiently for the family ahead of her to place their order.

Mari settled for a blackberry shake. By the time she went back outside, Bryce had finished eating. Before she could join him in his car, he wadded up his food wrappers and opened his door.

Waiting for him to make a move, she wrapped her lips around her straw in an attempt to drink the thick milkshake. His eyes darkened as he watched her and a muscle jumped in his cheek. Encouraged by his reaction, she tipped back her head and batted her eyes.

"Why don't you come home with me?" she asked softly. "We can…talk."

At this point, she didn't care that he knew exactly what she was suggesting. Ever since she had first spotted him sitting in his car, heat had spread through her like a fever. The cold milkshake was doing nothing to cool it.

For a moment, an answering spark flared in his eyes. His gaze dropped to her mouth, searing it. His fingers flexed and she thought he might reach for her.

His withdrawal was palpable. A shutter dropped down over his eyes and his face seemed to harden. He glanced at the clock on his dash. "I've got an errand to run."

Unwilling to give up, she felt like a beggar looking for crumbs as she bent down. "Could you come by later?"

"I'll try," he said hoarsely.

Chapter Ten

When Bryce drove away from South Junction Burgers, his hands were wrapped around the wheel so tightly that his fingers would probably leave grooves. His foot wanted to press the accelerator to the floor, leaving a patch of rubber on the street. Doing so might blow off some of his immediate frustration, but he'd probably get pulled over for road rage. That would be damned embarrassing.

He had been around long enough to know when a woman was sending out signals. Even though he might be too thick-witted to work out the purpose behind Mari's invitation, there was no mistaking the slow burn of her gaze or the husky catch to her voice.

When she had sashayed out of the burger joint with her mouth wrapped around the straw to her milk-shake, he'd nearly crawled through his car window to get to her.

Now that they were adults, the promise smoldering between them as teenagers was a fire that burned out of control whenever they were together. He wanted nothing more than to follow her home and take her to bed, to bury himself so deeply inside her that they would both be able to forget everything else going on around them.

Bryce's X-rated thoughts were interrupted by a request for assistance at the scene of an apparent homicide at the other end of the county. The victim, a young homeless man, made Bryce think of Joey.

After several hours spent canvassing witnesses, Bryce was able to leave. On his way to Crystal's house, he pulled over to the curb to again call his brother. Joey didn't answer, so Bryce left another message.

Crystal lived in an older section of town. Despite its closeness to the medical complex, this particular area was losing its struggle against urban decay.

Beneath the glow from the streetlights, her block was a jumble of mismatched houses, shabby multi-plexes and odd-size buildings. Yards were cluttered and full of weeds, fences were falling down and what grass there once was had dried up or been choked out by weeds. A sense of weary despair hung over the neighborhood like a toxic cloud. Even the parked cars looked worn-out.

He was surprised that a nurse, even one raising a child alone, couldn't afford to live somewhere a bit nicer. Perhaps she liked the convenience of being close to work.

Watching the address numbers, he turned into the parking lot of a square, ugly box of an apartment house. Crystal's unit was on the first floor, in a row of nearly identical square windows and faded pink doors with aluminum screens.

He could hear music from somewhere above and the noise of a nearby television. A car horn sounded from down the street. Her apartment was dark and the numbered parking spot in front of it was empty. A dead plant in a plastic pot sat by the door. Next to it was a crumpled candy wrapper and a toy truck with a missing wheel. It must belong to her little boy.

He rang the bell, just in case someone was home, but it echoed inside with a hollow sound. Apparently Nurse Hendrix was taking advantage of her freedom while her child was out of town.

Bryce could have asked Mari if she knew Crystal's hours, but the clinic staff was large enough that she probably didn't, and questions would have made her curious. He wasn't ready to jack up her hopes for nothing.

Or to crush his own. He wished Joey would return his call. Bryce would like nothing more than to hear that Joey's ex-girlfriend's last name had matched some other rock musician's. Crystal Starr?

He was tempted to question her neighbors, but he didn't want her tipped off that someone from the sheriff's department had been snooping around. In his slacks and lightweight jacket, he could be mistaken for a salesman or a bill collector.

As he turned, he saw an eye staring back at him through the partly opened door of the next apartment. It opened a little wider.

"Help you?" asked a stooped, elderly man with a scratchy voice.

Bryce stuck his hands into the pockets of his slacks. "Seen Ms. Hendrix?"

"She hasn't been around."

Before Bryce could ask if he meant today or this month, the man shut his door with a solid thud.

Frustration curdled Bryce's gut as he walked back to his car. For this he'd turned down Mari?

A pair of headlights turned into the parking lot, but the vehicle went in the opposite direction. Rap music blared from its stereo despite the late hour.

Bryce would have to come back later. Until he either talked to Crystal or Joey came out of hiding, there was nothing left for him to do. His hands were tied.

Before he slid behind the wheel, he glanced at his watch. He would have sent up a silent prayer that Mari would still be waiting, but the type of earthy request he had in mind seemed unsuitable for a heavenly plea. Wishing on a star was too G-rated, so he settled for a fervent hope.

Once again he felt like burning rubber in a race to reach her as quickly as possible, before she changed her mind and went to bed alone. Once again he kept his speed beneath the legal limit, but it felt as though his car was crawling.

Bryce's head was spinning, full of questions he couldn't answer and feelings he didn't understand. Figuring out what to say when he got to her condo was going to fill every moment that it took him to drive across town.

As it turned out, when she opened the door and he got a look at the way she was dressed, he nearly forgot how to talk at all.

Earlier that evening Mari had been pacing restlessly, refusing to count down the hours until Bryce's deadline ran out and Sheriff Remington removed him from the case. If Bryce came back, she was going to do her best to distract both him and herself from this sword of Damocles that had hung over their heads for too many weeks.

She had no doubt that Bryce wanted her. Lust burned between them like a forest fire raging out of control. Anything more complicated than desire would just have to wait.

When the door chimes finally sounded, she looked through the peephole to make sure it was Bryce and not her underage neighbor who stood outside. If Jordan got a glimpse of her dressed like this, she really would have legal trouble.

The hour was late enough for traffic to be infrequent and it was unlikely that her doorway could be seen from the street. Taking a deep breath, she moistened her lips with the tip of her tongue. What was worth doing, she recited silently as she swung the door open wide, was worth doing well. Striking a pose she hoped was effective, she rested her upraised arm along the jamb.

"Hey, big fella," she purred. "What took you so long?"

Bryce's reaction to the sheer black teddy, garter belt and fishnet hose was worth every dollar she'd paid for the outfit at an exclusive Lexington boutique. If he'd been chewing gum, she had no doubt that he would have swallowed it.

His eyes bugged out. His mouth dropped open. For once Detective Collins was speechless.

Despite his initial reaction, he had a cop's reflexes.

"Get inside before someone sees you," he barked, holding open his jacket to shield her from the street.

Before she could complain about his bossy attitude, he'd slammed the door behind him and pinned her against it, plastering his body to hers. His mouth was hot and his hands were everywhere.

Each move he made was that of a frustrated male who'd been pushed too far—and every woman's X-rated fantasy. Mari gave herself up willingly to the passion crackling between them. If she didn't end up with carpet burns on some part of her anatomy, she would be surprised.

Bryce was tied up for most of the next day assisting in the murder investigation of the homeless man, who had been stabbed. There was no apparent witnesses and a search for the weapon was fruitless.

When Bryce finally finished his report late in the afternoon, he headed for the Foster Clinic. His deadline on the Orcadol case ticked in his head like the timer on a bomb.

"Crystal is off today. Could someone else help you?" asked Heather, the young receptionist. She had changed her hair color from blue to an intense shade of pink, but she still regarded Bryce with a trace of suspicion.

"Nurse Hendrix may have witnessed a traffic accident," he lied smoothly. "Do you have any idea where I might catch her?"

"She mentioned that she planned on spending the day getting caught up on housework," Heather replied. "Her shift tomorrow starts at 8:00 a.m., so you can probably talk to her then."

"Thanks for your help." Bryce had no intention of waiting until the next morning. He drove directly back to the apartment building he'd last checked out after leaving Mari's condo at dawn that morning.

Each time they made love was more intense and more satisfying than the last. His first sight of her last night, draped in the doorway in that black getup, had stripped his mind of coherent thought.

When he had finally kissed her goodbye afterward, he realized how much she had always meant to him—and still did.

He had thought their shared history would have somehow immunized him from emotional involvement. How wrong he had been. Losing Mari for the second time might be more than his poor heart would be able to survive. The notion scared the hell out of him.

Focusing on the duty at hand, Bryce saw that Crystal's reserved spot was still empty. With a sigh of resignation, he parked along the street where he had a clear view of her unit and settled in to wait for her to show up.

Mari checked her cell phone for messages as she drove back to Binghamton. She'd accompanied one of the young midwives on a home visit, but Mari had taken her own car in case Bryce called with news. The midwife was inexperienced, but the mother's third baby, an eight-pound girl, had made her debut into the world without complications.

On the seat next to Mari was a pile of paperwork from her in-basket. She would review it at home, where she could work without interruptions.

Briefly she considered going by the clinic, but she had no reason to stop. Bryce could reach her at the condo. After last night, she doubted that he would forget where she lived. By the time he'd crawled out of her bed, there was a hint of light in the eastern sky. He'd been no more ready to leave than she was to let him go, but he had promised to stay in contact.

She smothered a yawn as she drove. The peace and quiet of her condo and her cat beckoned, too tempting to resist. She had the makings of a salad, an opened bottle of Merlot and the latest Tom Hanks movie that she'd rented. Perhaps the combination would take her mind off Bryce, the fast-approaching deadline and the longing to be with him that was getting harder to ignore each day—and night.

After she got home and went through the familiar routine of feeding Lennox and herself, she poured a second glass of wine—her absolute limit—and took the stack of papers to her home office. Two walls were lined with floor-to-ceiling bookcases containing everything from weighty medical tomes to gardening books and paperback romances.

The window seat was one of Lennox's favorite spots for his daily naps. It faced the common area she shared with the other residents. They had all worked to turn the sheltered space into a well-tended garden that attracted a variety of birds and butterflies. Among the plantings were a birdbath, a sundial and a rustic bench for relaxing.

Kicking off her shoes, Mari turned on the stereo and sat down at the teak rolltop desk, a present from her father. It had numerous drawers and cubbyholes surrounding a work surface that was wide enough for both her computer keyboard and a space for shuffling papers.

Quickly she leafed through the staff requests, reports and other forms that needed her approval.

Next in the pile was a reminder notice from the company that supplied prescription drugs to the clinic pharmacy.

She was relieved to see that delivery of the back-ordered Orcadol was scheduled for this evening. Their supply was nearly gone. As always, the security guard, a trusted longtime employee, would be on hand to receive it.

An echo of something about another big shipment niggled in her mind. A whispered remark. Where had she been at the time, she wondered idly.

Not the clinic, she mused. Not a restaurant and not an overheard cell-phone conversation. She could hear the sound in her head, two muffled, secretive male voices, but she couldn't picture the speakers.

Like an elusive song title or a half-remembered name, the fragment would bug her until it came to her. Drumming her fingers on the desk pad, she closed her eyes and thought hard.

Suddenly her eyes flew open as it hit her. She had been waiting for Bryce in the interrogation room, too nervous to pay full attention to what she heard through the partly open door. It was the men's furtive voices that had made an impression.

Had they been discussing something illegal, like drugs? Considering the location, there was certainly a possibility. What if they were talking about Orchid and she had overheard a key bit of information without even realizing it? She had to tell Bryce.

Mari reached for the phone, but then she hesitated. She wasn't able to describe the men. For all she knew, they could be deputies, snitches or crooks. They had been discussing some kind of big shipment, which wasn't in itself a crime. What were the odds that she had very conveniently overheard a conversation that had something to do with the stolen Orcadol?

Not very likely.

Did she want to run the risk of Bryce seeing her as the kind of woman who would use any reason, even a fabricated one, as an excuse to call him?

If the comment she had overheard turned out to be a valuable clue, if there really was a connection between the Orcadol that had been stolen and tonight's delivery, she would be instrumental in solving the case and clearing her name! She could use her resulting fifteen minutes of fame to spread the word about the research facility!

The entire idea was nuts, of course. Coincidences like that didn't just happen. On the other hand, what could it hurt to drive by the clinic and check out the delivery? If she saw anything at all suspicious, she would call Bryce on her cell.

Pleased with her game plan, Mari grabbed her purse and keys. Lennox followed her to the entry, meowing insistently.

Before she opened the door, Mari stopped to pat the cat's head.

"If Detective Collins calls," she said with a smile, "tell him I'm on a case."

Bryce watched a dusty green coupe pull into Crystal's reserved spot. A pretty young blonde, just Joey's type, got out and glanced around as though she was nervous, but she didn't notice Bryce sitting across the street. He waited until she had gone inside and closed the door before he walked across the parking lot.

After the second time he rang her bell, the door finally opened with the security chain in place. The same young blonde peered at him through the crack.

"Yes?"

Bryce held up his badge so she could see it.

"Ms. Hendrix, I'm Detective Collins. I understand you know my younger brother, Joey."

Perhaps she would assume that Bryce was here because of him. As long as the connection got Bryce inside without a hassle, he didn't care what she thought.

"Oh, dear Lord!" she cried.

The strength of her reaction startled him as she slammed the door and freed the chain. When she flung it back open, he saw that her face was already beginning to show the signs of a difficult life.

"Is Ryan all right?" she asked, clutching at Bryce. "He hasn't been hurt, has he?"

Bryce thought the boy was visiting his father in the Midwest. What the hell was going on here, and how was Joey involved? A cop's nose for trouble told Bryce he wasn't going to like what he was about to find out.

"May I come inside?" he asked.

"Oh, yes, of course." She nearly jumped out of his way, her movements as nervous as those of a bird being stalked by a hungry cat.

Was he going to find out the cat was his brother?

Bryce opened the screen and stepped into the apartment.

"What's happened to my baby?" she asked as soon as he shut the door behind him. She pressed the knuckles of one hand to her trembling mouth as her eyes filled with tears. "Please, please tell me!"

Afraid she would become too hysterical to answer his questions, Bryce touched her thin shoulder in an attempt to calm her. She was vibrating with tension.

"As far as I know, your son is fine," he said in his most reassuring voice. "You and I need to talk."

He glanced around the small room. It opened onto a dining area and a kitchenette with a view of the parking lot and the street. Other than the child's drawings taped on the front of the refrigerator, there was nothing to distinguish the apartment from dozens like it.

"You're not here about Ryan?" Crystal asked, her expression closing up.

Slowly Bryce shook his head. What had Joey gotten himself into and where was Ryan?

"Then I can't talk to you." She hugged herself as though she was afraid of flying apart. "You have to go right now!"

Instead of leaving, Bryce walked over to the couch. "May I?" He sat down without waiting for her reply.

She sidled up to the front window, clutching a locket she wore around her neck, and glanced outside. "Why are you here?"

"Is your son visiting his father?" Bryce asked. "If

you tell me that he is, Ms. Hendrix, I'll need your ex-husband's number in order to verify the information.''

For a moment she stared down at him resentfully, her mouth working, and then she squeezed her eyes shut. A single tear trickled down her pale cheek. Like a puppet whose strings had been cut, she collapsed abruptly onto a straight chair opposite him. More tears flowed.

''He swore that if I talked to anyone, he'd hurt my little boy,'' she whispered. ''You tell him that I've kept my mouth shut, just like he said.''

Bryce's stomach dropped like a stone. ''*Who* told you that?''

Her hands were clasped together so tightly her knuckles were bone white. ''My ex-boyfriend, Joey Collins.''

Her words were like blows that Bryce wanted to evade, but couldn't. He had known Joey had faults, but was he really capable of doing what she claimed?

With a few chilling words, the woman sitting across from Bryce had altered his world. If what she said was true, the brother he loved was a coldhearted stranger.

When Bryce tried to breathe, he felt as though a heavy weight was pressing down on his chest. He wanted to cover Crystal's mouth with his hand to stop the flow of ugly words. Part of him longed to curl up in a protective ball, to close his eyes and ears so that he didn't have to deal with what she was saying.

That wasn't Bryce's style. He faced trouble head-on.

What he had to do was to figure out what was going on so he could contain the situation. He had one shot to reel in Joey and find that little boy.

Forcing himself to put aside the sick dread boiling up in his gut, Bryce took out his notebook and pen.

"Do you have any idea where Joey could be holding your son?" he asked.

Eyes wide, she shook her head. If anything, she had turned even paler.

"Okay, start from the beginning." Bryce kept his voice steady, even though he felt like screaming. "Don't leave anything out."

"Will I go to jail?" she asked hoarsely. "If I get arrested, I'll lose custody. Ryan will have to live with his father in Ohio, and I'll never see him again."

"Don't worry about that now." Bryce struggled for patience.

He didn't have much time before he'd be forced to start making phone calls. He knew the procedure, but the more people who got involved, the harder it would be to keep the danger to everyone involved from escalating.

"Why did Joey take your little boy?" he asked.

"He was always complaining about the Binghams." Her voice was so soft that Bryce had to lean forward to hear her. "He blames them for everything that's ever gone wrong in his life."

"I know that," he replied. "We may not have a lot of time, Ms. Hendrix. What was Joey trying to get you to do?"

Again the tears began to flow.

"At first he just asked me to steal some Orcadol for him. I didn't want to do it, but he kept pushing me." She pulled a tissue from the box on a nearby table and blotted her eyes. "I didn't think that would be so bad as long as I put another painkiller in its place."

She was a nurse, so she should have known better. A woman had died and several more became ill or suffered allergic reactions to the drug she had substituted.

"Go on," he prodded, selfishly wanting to hurry her, but knowing that he couldn't or she might clam up. He was also beginning to suspect that Crystal wasn't quite the innocent victim she was attempting to portray.

"After a while I got scared that someone would see me switching the drugs," she said, "especially after Dr. Bingham started asking all of us if we had noticed anything suspicious."

Bryce did his best to appear sympathetic. "Then what happened?"

"After a couple of Joey's buddies got caught selling Orchid, I told him I wanted out. He was really upset and he threatened to get me fired. I told him we'd be getting a new shipment of it, and that's when he decided to make a big score." She pressed the heels of her hands to her temples. "I didn't want to help him, so he took Ryan. I've been making excuses to my ex, but he's getting impatient, too."

"What are you supposed to do in order to keep Ryan safe?" Bryce asked.

"I don't know if I can trust you," she wailed. "He's your brother, and he's got my baby."

Bryce reached out to take her hand. It was icy cold.

"I took an oath to uphold the law," he said firmly, as much to remind himself of his duty, as well as to convince her. "I'll do everything I can to bring your boy back to you unhurt, but you have to trust me, Crystal. Otherwise I can't promise you anything."

She studied his face for what seemed like an eternity.

"He wanted the security code to the pharmacy. I had to give it to him."

Bryce wasn't interested right now in how she had gotten the code. He would deal with the security breach later.

"Is he planning to rob the clinic pharmacy?" He struggled to block out his personal feelings.

"Not exactly. A truck is supposed to make a delivery this evening. I guess he's going to pretend that he works there so he can steal the shipment of Orcadol."

All his life Joey had been impulsive and opportunistic, but if he thought he'd be able to pull off such a simplistic plan and stick the blame on Mari, he was a lot dumber than Bryce had ever realized. He had to find Joey and stop him.

"How many people are involved?"

Joey would have to face the consequences, of course. Bryce couldn't protect him. Right now Bryce's only purpose was to keep everyone safe.

"I don't know," she replied with a frown, but then

her expression brightened slightly. "He had me get him three jackets from the clinic laundry."

"Good girl," Bryce replied, his mind racing. "You stay here and don't talk to anyone, understand? Ryan's safety depends on my ability to stop Joey before whatever he's got planned goes down."

As soon as she gave him her word, making an X over her heart with her finger as a child would, he hurried to his car. He was reaching for the door handle when a chill went up his spine.

Mari had mentioned that she might stay late at the clinic in order to clear up some paperwork. She could be in danger!

He got behind the wheel and tried calling her, but her cell phone went straight to voice mail.

"If you're at the clinic, please leave immediately," he said as he turned his key in the ignition. "I'll explain later."

The next call he made, without a conscious choice, was to the dispatcher. Not even to spare his brother was Bryce willing to risk a little boy's safety, nor that of the woman who still owned Bryce's heart.

Chapter Eleven

Mari arrived at the clinic after hours. Through the front windows, the building appeared empty and the interior lights were dimmed. She had no idea what she'd expected to find, but nothing looked out of place.

Telling herself she had an overactive imagination, she drove around to the back. If she saw Frank, the security guard, she would ask if the delivery truck from the drug company had shown up yet.

A plain white van was backed up to the service entrance. Both the back door of the van and the heavy security door to the clinic were open, but there was no one in sight. Perhaps the driver and Frank were inside the building, dealing with the freight.

A shiver of nervousness, like icy fingertips, ran up Mari's spine. Something didn't feel right. Maybe coming here by herself hadn't been smart.

The van blocked the driveway. As she started to turn her car around, she reached for her cell phone to call Bryce.

She pressed the buttons, but nothing happened. When she glanced down, she remembered that she had meant to charge the battery last night. Somewhere between her bubble bath and Bryce's arrival, mundane chores had slipped her mind. Now, the phone was dead.

She was shifting out of Reverse when a man she had never seen before came through the door to the clinic. Wearing a lab coat and a knit cap, he appeared as surprised as Mari. In thc few seconds they stared at each other, she realized that he was dressed all wrong. Under the lab coat he wore faded jeans and heavy work boots.

Before she could force her suddenly frozen muscles to react so she could remove her foot from the brake, the man stepped in front of her car. In order to leave, she'd have to deliberately run him down.

What had she been thinking to come here alone? She should have followed her instinct and called Bryce!

Trying to appear confused and nonthreatening, she plastered a confused smile on her face. ''I think I took a wrong turn,'' she said through her open window. ''I'm looking for parking.''

The man scowled and pointed impatiently in the wrong direction. ''It's over that way.''

''Thanks. My mistake.'' She waited impatiently for him to get out of her way. Before he did, two more men came outside, both of them wearing lab coats. One was wheeling a hand truck stacked with small cartons. The other was carrying a gun.

Mari recognized him instantly. As she stared in openmouthed shock, he saw her, too, and raised his gun. Holding it with both hands, he aimed straight at her through the open car window.

''So we meet again, Dr. Bingham!'' Joey Collins exclaimed. ''What a shame you had to show up before we finished.''

Mari's mind was blank with fear. She had never before stared down the barrel of a gun, and Joey's cheerful grin did nothing to soften the flat, reptilian stare of his eyes. She struggled to overcome the terror that gripped her. Somehow she had to talk her way out of this so she could get to a phone.

''I'd appreciate it if you'd get out of the car.'' Joey motioned with the gun. ''Keep your hands where I can see them, and don't even think about doing anything stupid, okay?''

''What are you doing here?'' she blurted, even though it was obvious. The cartons they were loading into the van were full of prescription drugs.

''Don't ask a bunch of dumb questions!'' His voice

cracked as it got louder. "I'm in charge now, so just do what you're told!" he screamed.

All she could think as she set the brake, fumbling with it the first time so that she had to try again, was that she would be able to identify him. Did that mean he would have to kill her?

When she got out of the car, her knees shook so hard that she clung to the door handle to keep from falling.

"What have you done with Frank?" she asked through clenched teeth. She needed to stall on the slim chance that someone, somehow, would notice what was going on and call 911.

Joey frowned. "Oh, you mean the rent-a-cop? Don't worry, he'll be okay. We locked him in a closet."

Was he telling the truth, or was Frank lying somewhere inside the clinic, disabled by a gunshot wound or a blow to the head? The poor man didn't even carry a weapon.

Joey glanced at his accomplice. "Don't just stand there, Butch! Move the car out of the way so we can get out of here. Hurry up!"

If only Mari could think of something that might influence Joey in some way. For Bryce's sake, as well as her own, she had to try.

"If you turn yourself in, I'll help you in any way I can," she promised.

"Yeah, your family's big on helping people," Joey sneered.

Butch looked her over with a grin that showed dirty, broken teeth. "We should take her with us."

Mari thought her heart would stop.

"Never mind," Joey snarled. "Get the rest of the stuff loaded. Come on, move!"

Butch glared resentfully, but he did as he was told. The third man must have gone back inside.

"Just lock me inside with Frank," Mari pleaded as Joey darted a nervous glance toward the van. "You'll have plenty of time to get away before anyone finds us."

"Shut up!" he screamed. "You're not the boss. That fancy medical degree that you dumped my brother for isn't going to help you now."

"I didn't dump him," she protested without thinking.

"Hurry up!" he shouted again as Butch loaded more boxes into the back of the van. "We gotta get out of here!"

"I got a couple more cartons."

The third man appeared briefly with a bank-deposit bag that he tossed onto the seat before following Butch back inside the building.

They didn't seem very organized, Mari thought distractedly.

"I'll forget I ever saw you," she pleaded. "Who'd believe me? Everyone thinks I'm the one who's been stealing the drugs all along."

Joey giggled, sounding a little crazy. "Framing you was my idea. I'll have a fortune in Orchid and you'll get blamed. Maybe you'll even go to prison." His eyes seemed to burn. "It's what you deserve."

"That was pretty clever," she agreed, forcing her voice to be calm as she stared at his finger on the trigger. "But you'll ruin it if you hurt me."

Butch hurried back out with another box. It slipped from his hands, breaking open when it hit the ground. Swearing, he kicked it aside and the contents spilled out.

Joey lifted the gun higher, pointing it straight at Mari's head. "You're wrong," he said harshly. "People will think we argued over the size of your cut."

He was probably right. Reading the violence in his expression, she realized that she was about to pay a huge price for her pride. Her heart stuttered in her chest. How foolish of her to worry about what Bryce might have thought if she had called him.

She hated the idea of never seeing him again! If she was going to die, her biggest regret was that he would never know how she felt.

She swallowed hard. "When you see Bryce, would you tell him that I love him?"

Joey's face went blank with surprise and his gun hand sagged. "What?"

"Tell him—"

"Drop the gun, bro."

Bryce! For a moment, Mari thought she was imagining the sound of his voice, but then the second man straightened abruptly and raised his hands.

"Oh, man," Joey wailed, swinging the gun back

and forth erratically. "Why the hell did you have to show up?"

Mari risked a quick glance over her shoulder. Even with a gun in his hand and a fierce scowl, Bryce looked wonderful.

"Nobody move!" Joey screamed. He raked his free hand through his hair so it stood on end, making him appear more disturbed than ever. He must be using some of the drugs himself.

"Someone's got to keep an eye on you, bro," Bryce said calmly. He moved closer so that Mari could see him from the corner of her eye. "Just take it easy."

Suddenly Mari remembered the third accomplice. Before she could warn Bryce, he appeared from behind the van, gun aimed at Bryce.

"No!" Joey lunged as the gun went off.

Mari screamed as Bryce grunted and doubled over. He fell to his knees, clutching his chest. Forgetting everything else, she ran to him as he collapsed on the ground, blood oozing between his fingers.

Oh, God, oh, God, she recited silently, fighting hysteria. He stared up at her, his eyes glazed with shock, but at least he was still alive.

He needed her medical expertise, not her tears. "Stay with me," she told him, forcing calmness into her voice. "You're going to be fine."

The hospital, right on the other side of the clinic, might as well have been miles away as she struggled to stop the bleeding.

"Marigold, you okay?" he whispered, slurring the words.

"I'm fine." She fought back a fresh sob, hiding her fear. "Save your strength."

A police siren wailed in the distance.

"Glad…you're…doc-tor." His eyelids drooped.

She glared up at Joey, who stared down at Bryce with his gun dangling at his side. His face was pale and beaded with perspiration, his expression one of disbelief.

"How could you let this happen?" Mari demanded.

He gave her a stricken look and then he spun away. "Come on," he screamed. "Let's go, let's get out of here!"

The siren grew louder. Another shot was fired, followed by shouting, but she paid no attention. Bryce had lost consciousness.

She glanced up to see a pair of uniformed deputies standing in front of her, weapons drawn, and two of the thieves with their hands up.

"I need help here," she cried. "Officer down!"

Bryce was trapped in an endless loop of disturbing dreams, like being in a fun house with no way of escape. Each time he struggled to find an exit, exhaustion dragged at him.

Why was he so tired? Had he been drugged? He attempted to open his eyes, but his lids were too heavy.

Finally sounds began to filter through the oppressive cloud weighing him down. They were muted—a ringing phone, distant voices, a door slamming. At least they were real.

Concentrating hard, he pried open his eyes. The light was dim, but he was surprised it was no longer night. The room he found himself in was unfamiliar. The bed had a side railing and there was an IV taped to his arm, but at least he wasn't restrained.

While he was deciding whether or not to rip out the needle, he turned his head and saw Mari curled up in a chair next to the bed with her eyes closed. Relief shuddered through him, followed by a rush of gratitude.

As though she could sense him looking at her, she stirred and opened her eyes. Bryce tried to sit up, but pain smacked him back down. His shoulder was bandaged.

"You're awake," Mari exclaimed softly.

Even though she was clearly exhausted, she didn't appear to be injured and she looked like an angel to him. He couldn't remember ever being so happy to see anyone.

"How are you feeling?" she asked, leaning closer to brush his cheek lightly with her fingertips.

"Kind of spaced out." His mouth was dry and his tongue felt swollen to twice its normal size. "You're okay?" he croaked.

She nodded. "Thanks to you."

She poured him some water in a plastic cup. After

she had carefully raised the head of the bed, she held the cup for him while he drank through a straw.

"Why am I here?" he asked.

She brushed the hair back from his forehead, and he realized that she had changed into scrubs.

"You had surgery to remove a bullet from your shoulder. After you were shot, you lost a fair amount of blood." Her smile wavered, and she blinked hard. "The surgeon will be in to see you, but there were no signs of permanent damage. After some physical therapy, you'll be as good as new."

He glanced away, grateful to hear that his career wasn't over. He had so many questions.

"Your parents were here for a while, but I sent them home," she added. "I promised that you'd call as soon as you're able."

"Yeah, sure." His mom would be worried. She was always afraid he'd get hurt.

"You know the sheriff wants to talk to you, too," Mari said, touching his good arm.

Bryce closed his eyes as bits and pieces came flooding back. Panic welled up inside him. He did not want to talk about how his own brother had tried to kill him.

"I'm tired now," he muttered. "I need to rest."

He waited, scarcely breathing, for her to leave. A memory teased the edge of his consciousness, something important he'd heard her say. The words remained just beyond his reach.

"Bryce," she whispered, "do you know that you're a hero?"

His eyes flew back open. "How can you say that after I let you down?" he demanded harshly. "Look what I put you through for all these weeks, hounding you the way I did."

"It wasn't your fault," she protested. "You were just doing your job."

"Was anyone else hurt?" he was almost afraid to ask. What if Joey was dead?

"No," she replied quickly. "Only you, and you'll be fine. The other deputies you called were delayed by a collision that blocked one of the main intersections downtown, but they arrived right after you got shot. They found Frank, the clinic security guard, trussed up with tape and locked in a broom closet. I guess he was pretty mad."

"So Joey's in jail?" Bryce could still picture his brother with his gun pointed straight at Bryce's heart. He didn't know if he would ever be able to get past it, that and endangering Mari.

She hesitated, as though she didn't know quite what to say.

Bryce shifted, ignoring the pain, and grabbed her wrist. "Tell me!" he demanded. "I want to know where he is."

A car drove by with its stereo blasting. It was hard for him to believe that outside the building, life went on as usual.

Mari turned her hand over, lacing her fingers with his.

"When the deputies arrived, you were bleeding all over the place and there was a lot of confusion. The other two men were apprehended, but somehow Joey managed to escape."

"He got away?" Bryce was dumbfounded. He had promised Crystal he would bring Ryan back to her, so he had let her down, too.

"Joey's got Crystal's little boy. I've got to tell the sheriff."

He tried to sit up again, but Mari pushed him gently back down.

"They already know about Ryan. As soon as Crystal heard the news report about the shooting, she went downtown and confessed everything."

Bryce gulped in a deep breath. "I hope the kid's okay. Joey wouldn't..." His voice broke off. He had no idea how far Joey would go to fulfill his twisted need for revenge.

"They'll be okay, both of them," Mari said softly.

"He's always blamed your family for everything wrong in his life," Bryce muttered, shaking his head. "Not too long ago he was bragging about some big deal. He promised to buy me a car when it went down, but he was usually drunk or high, so I never paid any attention." He stared vacantly. "I should have listened."

She squeezed their linked hands. "It's okay." Her

voice was soothing, as though she were speaking to a child. "It will all work out."

"You don't know that!" Bryce jerked away from her. "My own brother shot me. How do you get around something like that?" he choked as his vision blurred.

"No, no, you're wrong." She leaned closer, forcing him to look at her. "Your brother didn't shoot you, sweetie. It was one of the other men."

"Are you sure?"

"I witnessed it, remember?" she asked dryly. "If Joey hadn't shouted and managed to hit the other man's arm right when he fired, who knows what might have happened?" Her eyes grew moist. "There's a good chance that Joey actually saved your sorry butt," she added.

Bryce searched her face suspiciously, looking for signs that she wasn't telling the truth. She was pale, but her gaze was steady on his.

"Thanks for telling me," he whispered. "It means a lot."

"I suppose it would be pointless to suggest that you come home with us and get some rest," Cecilia said dryly.

She and Geoff sat with Mari in the cafeteria. They had arrived shortly after her frantic phone call, and they had been at the hospital ever since. Myrtle had come by to reassure herself that Mari was still in one piece, and Kyle had looked in on her, as had many of her co-workers. All she really cared about was Bryce's progress. How awful for him that his brother had turned out to be the one responsible for so much suffering.

A plate of toast and scrambled eggs sat untouched in front of her as she sipped her black coffee. She was still struggling to absorb everything that had taken place, and to deal with her reactions.

"Don't bother giving my sister advice," Geoff huffed, glancing at his wife. "Mari's head is as hard as granite."

"You men just don't get it," Cecilia retorted with a secretive wink at Mari.

She just smiled tiredly. Except for the nap she'd taken in the chair while Bryce recovered, she had been up all night. Adrenaline had kept her going, that and sheer will.

Despite her medical training, until Bryce had finally regained consciousness, she'd been gripped by bone-deep fear that something terrible and unexpected could still happen to him.

"I'm going back upstairs," she said abruptly, setting aside her half-full mug and pushing back her chair. "The sheriff must be done talking to Bryce by now."

"You didn't eat a thing," Cecilia exclaimed. "At least take a slice of toast with you or you'll be useless to him."

"Your cop is going to be fine," Geoff added gruffly. He and Mari had talked a little bit, and he seemed willing to revise his opinion about Bryce. "There were a half dozen of his buddies waiting in the hall when we dragged you out of his room."

"Thanks for breakfast." Mari bent to kiss each of their cheeks. "And thanks for coming. I'll call you later."

When she got back upstairs, Sheriff Remington was just coming out of Bryce's room. In his dress uniform, with his wiry build, weathered complexion and silver hair, the sheriff exuded an air of reassurance.

He had questioned Mari earlier and now he greeted her again with a firm handshake and a campaign-worthy smile.

"I don't think you'll have to worry about any charges being filed against you," he said. "I hope you understand that we were only following procedure."

"Of course." She glanced impatiently at the door to Bryce's room. "Is he okay?"

He nodded. "Detective Collins is one of my best men. I'm recommending him for a citation." His expression turned solemn. "We found Joey Collins's car abandoned on the edge of town. There was no sign of him or Ryan Hendrix, but we'll get them."

"I'm sure you will," Mari agreed, and then she excused herself to visit Bryce.

She had come too close to losing him, so she wanted to spend as much time with him as she could while he was still more or less captive. Who knew what would happen once he was released.

When she pushed open the door and went inside, he was propped up in bed.

"Hi," Bryce said, smiling through his obvious fatigue. "I was hoping you'd come back."

"Are you hungry?" she asked. "Lunch won't be served for a while, but I can bring you a tray from downstairs."

He shook his head. "You and I need to talk."

"Okay." Mari approached the bed warily and sat down in the chair.

"Did you mean what you told Joey?" he asked bluntly.

Her heart sank. She'd been hoping that Bryce either hadn't overheard her asking Joey to tell him that she loved him, or that all the drugs in his system would have blotted it from his mind.

Now she could feel a blush spread over her face, turning her cheeks bright red. Her first impulse was to make excuses. She could say that her words had been a desperate, although far-fetched, attempt to stall for time in the hopes of being rescued.

She studied the beloved face of the man she had come so close to losing. As she did, she remembered with perfect clarity the aching regret she had felt when she spoke those words. She couldn't turn around and deny them now.

Glancing down at her tightly clasped hands, she cleared her throat. "I meant what I said." Her voice came out as a husky whisper. "I do love you."

Bryce's eyes widened. It was obvious that she had surprised him.

"Look, it's okay," she added quickly. "I don't expect you to say anything in return, especially while your system has been pumped full of painkillers. Don't worry about it."

Drawing in a quick breath, she rushed on. "Since you took a bullet for me, you probably deserve to know the rest. I never really got over you after we broke up." She laughed lightly, but it fell flat. "Oh, I tried to convince myself that I had, but no one else ever made me feel the way you did."

When he continued to stare, his silence unnerving, she babbled on.

"I don't regret that first night you and I spent in my office or the times we've been together since then, but I don't want you to think that I expect anything from you, because I don't."

Later on, when she wasn't so tired and she'd had time to recall exactly what she was saying now, she would no doubt deeply regret her loose tongue.

"I'll probably have to leave town after this," she muttered darkly, not realizing that she'd spoken out loud.

"Then we'd both be unhappy." His voice curled around her like black velvet. "That wouldn't make much sense, Marigold."

Mari stared. Were her ears hallucinating? Was that even physically possible? "What do you mean?"

"I never stopped loving you," he said bluntly.

"Not from the first time we went to the spring hop together, and not one day since then."

For a moment, Mari couldn't seem to breathe. She had never dreamed she would hear him say that again. Then the reality of their situation snapped her back like a rubber band.

"Then why did you break up with me?" she demanded.

"Technically, we broke up with each other," he said mildly. "You left without me, and I stayed behind."

"You knew that I wanted to be a doctor," she reminded him. "I had no choice but to go. Now answer my question."

He sat back against his pillows with a sigh, pinching the bridge of his nose with the thumb and finger of his good hand. "I was afraid you'd get around to asking me someday."

"Sounds like you've had a lot of time to contemplate your reply," she replied a little sharply.

If he tried to convince her that it had been a simple misunderstanding, she would probably strangle him with the IV tubing. Nothing between them had ever been uncomplicated.

"Look," he said, "there was no way my family could afford to send me to college. My grades weren't high enough for a scholarship, and I wasn't that good a ballplayer."

It was her turn to let her mouth drop open.

"That's it?" she nearly screeched before she lowered her voice. "That's *it?*" she hissed again. "Why didn't you *tell* me?"

As far as she could recall, the subject of money had never once come up between them. She had assumed, as only someone who had never paid attention to the cost of *anything* in her young life could ever assume, that his parents had saved up enough money, or he would get a loan, or student aid or who knew what?

Like a spoiled princess, she realized with a sense of shame, she hadn't thought about his situation at all.

"As stupid as it sounds now," he said, "my pride wouldn't let me admit that my family couldn't afford something that must have seemed so basic to someone at your economic level. It would have been almost like admitting that we couldn't afford *food.*" He squirmed, and then he winced as though his shoulder had twinged. "I didn't want to embarrass my parents."

"Then why didn't you just come with me and get a job?" she asked, her insides quaking. Because he hadn't wanted to be with her bad enough.

He looked away, a muscle flexing in his cheek.

"I couldn't compete with the college boys you'd meet." His voice was so low that she had to lean down and listen carefully. "I knew that watching you fall for someone like that would rip my heart out."

She could tell that every word he said was sincere, painfully so.

"Oh, baby," she whispered, "I'm so sorry." What had her immaturity and his misplaced pride cost them? Could they ever regain it?

Then she remembered with a burst of warmth that he had said he loved her, too. Maybe there was still hope.

"Sounds like we've made some pretty big mistakes," he said gruffly. "Do you think you could ever be okay with my job? I don't think I could give it up."

She glanced at his bandaged shoulder. "Maybe while you're lying in bed with a bullet hole in you isn't the best time to ask that," she joked.

She realized with a jolt that he'd been serious because he didn't even crack a smile.

"I'm proud of what you do," she admitted. "I meant what I said before. You're my hero." She had to blink back sudden tears as she realized that what she'd said was true.

"How would you feel about having your sleep interrupted because I have to go deliver a baby?" she asked.

"You have the most important job in the world, bringing new life into it."

His words bowled her over. Before she could recover, he continued speaking.

"According to the sheriff, I haven't been fired yet," he said with a sudden gleam in his eyes. "I just want to warn you that once I'm back to full speed, there's something very important I'm going to be asking you.''

"Careful," she reminded him. "You're on drugs, so you may not want to say anything that could be construed as legally binding."

"It's not the drugs," he drawled. "I've felt this way for years."

For a moment, Mari's mind went blank and she had no idea what to say. Then an idea came to her mind.

"Why wait?" she challenged. "We've wasted too much time already."

"I want to do it right, and I'm in no shape to propose," he said, looking up at his IV pole.

"I am." With her heart thumping so hard she was afraid it might burst right out of her chest, she moved the chair out of the way and went down on one knee right next to the bed. She reached for Bryce's hand, gripping it tightly.

There was so much she wanted to say to him. Before she could figure out how to put everything she felt into words, the pure truth hit her like a ray of light.

He loved her, too.

She was so overcome with happiness that she could hardly speak. Tears clogged her throat and spilled from her eyes. Finally she realized there was no need for fancy words. The two of them would have a lifetime together for that.

"Honey, would you marry me?" she asked.

He squeezed her hand and his gaze shimmered suspiciously as he leaned closer.

"Absolutely," he said hoarsely. "I'm not letting you get away again."

Before he could seal their bargain with a kiss, the door behind Mari flew open and a nurse she didn't know walked into the room.

When the RN saw Mari on her knees, she stopped in her tracks and her eyes boggled.

"What's going on here?" she demanded with her hands on her hips. "This man is recovering from surgery."

"I lost something," Bryce said quickly. "Dr. Bingham was trying to find it for me."

Mari realized that he was trying to spare her from possibly embarrassing gossip. She met his gaze squarely for a moment and then she looked up at the nurse.

"My fiancé and I actually lost something of great value a long time ago," Mari explained as a sense of peace and contentment filled her. "Since I was determined never to risk it again, I just proposed to him and he's accepted."

"Oh," the nurse gasped, pressing one hand to her ample bosom, "that's such a beautiful sentiment, Dr. Bingham, Detective. Let me be the very first one to congratulate you both."

Before Mari could respond, Bryce thanked the nurse. Then he put his hand on Mari's chin and gently turned her head. His eyes were blazing with love as he took her mouth in a passionate kiss.

Faintly, she heard the nurse's voice as she departed down the hall.

"Annie! Ruth! You won't *believe* what just happened in 206!"

*   *   *   *   *

If you enjoyed what you just read,
then we've got an offer you can't resist!

Take 2 bestselling love stories FREE!

Plus get a FREE surprise gift!

Clip this page and mail it to Silhouette Reader Service™

IN U.S.A.	IN CANADA
3010 Walden Ave.	P.O. Box 609
P.O. Box 1867	Fort Erie, Ontario
Buffalo, N.Y. 14240-1867	L2A 5X3

YES! Please send me 2 free Silhouette Special Edition® novels and my free surprise gift. After receiving them, if I don't wish to receive anymore, I can return the shipping statement marked cancel. If I don't cancel, I will receive 6 brand-new novels every month, before they're available in stores! In the U.S.A., bill me at the bargain price of $3.99 plus 25¢ shipping and handling per book and applicable sales tax, if any*. In Canada, bill me at the bargain price of $4.74 plus 25¢ shipping and handling per book and applicable taxes**. That's the complete price and a savings of at least 10% off the cover prices—what a great deal! I understand that accepting the 2 free books and gift places me under no obligation ever to buy any books. I can always return a shipment and cancel at any time. Even if I never buy another book from Silhouette, the 2 free books and gift are mine to keep forever.

235 SDN DNUR
335 SDN DNUS

Name	(PLEASE PRINT)	
Address	Apt.#	
City	State/Prov.	Zip/Postal Code

* Terms and prices subject to change without notice. Sales tax applicable in N.Y.
** Canadian residents will be charged applicable provincial taxes and GST.
  All orders subject to approval. Offer limited to one per household and not valid to
  current Silhouette Special Edition® subscribers.
  ® are registered trademarks of Harlequin Books S.A., used under license.

SPED02   ©1998 Harlequin Enterprises Limited